M000188587

HYBRID VIGOR

JOHN LEE SCHNEIDER

SEVERED PRESS
HOBART TASMANIA

HYBRID VIGOR

Copyright © 2019 John Lee Schneider

WWW.SEVEREDPRESS.COM

ISBN: 978-1-925840-64-3

"You can walk around lions, and they may leave you alone. You can swim around man-eating sharks, and you might be alright. With crocodiles, it's different. There are rivers where, if you try to swim across, you just won't make it."

Quinton 'Crocodile' Marvin

CHAPTER 1

The swamp never gave up its dead.

But sometimes its denizens did.

And even though Daniel had grown up on the Everglades, this time they had coughed up something he had never seen before.

He steered the little outboard deftly through the marsh – they had been waiting for the rains to pass and the water to recede, but the estuaries were still flooded, disguising logs and other invisible hazards, so the going was slow – they puttered along, not straining the small motor – which was the only kind allowed this far out into the protected areas.

Of course, as park department ranger – ' Ranger Reid', as his office called him – Daniel could have by-passed those regulations, but best to lead by example – particularly in the company of his current passenger.

Jennifer – 'Jen' – her hair pulled back in a severe ponytail, with her last name, 'Summers', printed in no-nonsense capitals on the badge pinned to her work-shirt – sat poised at the bow of the boat, her light, athletic form recalling an image of an alert bird dog – a fond recollection, but the kind of remark Daniel had learned to leave unspoken.

Jen worked on the other side of the fence – private-sector(ish) conservationism – operating in tandem with Daniel's official office.

Technically, 'Gator Glades' was a theme-park – a local tourist attraction – but over the decades since its inception, it had evolved into a breeding and rehab facility for endangered local wildlife.

But while the park catered to birds and mammals, and swamp-critters of all kinds, the 'hook' that made it an attraction, was creepy-crawlies – reptilian in general and crocodilian in particular.

The public entrance said it all – a doorway built under a giant pair of crocodile jaws leading the public right down its gullet.

The owner was a man named Robert Wesley, a wealthy philanthropist-slash-local-politician, who had opened the facility back in the eighties – at the time, a purely profit-motivated endeavor – a 'croc park', originally purchased under a franchise deal with Sea World.

Wesley, however, had bought Gator Glades outright after Sea World's PR troubles, perhaps not coincidentally, at about the same time he had run for his first local office – a councilman position on which he campaigned primarily on local conservation, with particular emphasis on the rehabilitation of the Everglades.

With its primarily reptilian fare, Gator Glades didn't suffer the same negative attention as the sea parks, and Wesley continued to operate openly, even using the facility as a platform during the periodic formality of re-election.

It had been Wesley that had sent them out on the water today – after a long delay. The last series of storms had put the trip off nearly a week. The roads were still flooded, which was why they finally decided to go by boat.

It was also why the two of them were taking the trip instead of the police.

Ol' Bill's Cabin.

Ol' Bill was a local legend. And not in a good way.

The cabin was located on the very last of legal private property before the protected waters of Everglades National Park began. It was also accessible only by what could most-generously be described as 'unmaintained' roads – or else by the water itself.

The property also fell within the borders of one of the outer-limit non-towns that existed at the edge of the county lines – a fishing-shack motel, a bar, and supply store – nicknamed 'The Backwoods' by fishermen back in the day, and the name had stuck.

As Jen reported it, Wesley had been in contact with the local jurisdiction sheriff and was met with a marked lack of enthusiasm after Ol' Bill's name had come up.

The sheriff, an irascible, course-grained local named Barnes, had told Wesley he would "check on the old son of a bitch" and get back to him.

After a week passed and Barnes still had not called, Wesley had tried again, and this time he had been told – in impatient, and rather combative tones – that they couldn't get there, citing the flooded roads, and might not yet for a few more days.

Wesley had pointed out that this particular cabin in the woods might be a crime scene.

Barnes had replied curtly. "Then it still WILL be."

Rather than forcing the issue, Wesley had called the parks department, and Daniel had agreed to check out the cabin himself. With the little outboard in tow, he and Jen had driven out to the Backwoods before dawn, launching into the river off the township's single dock – the last construct of civilization until you reached the Gulf of Mexico on the far side of the 'glades.

And with that destination in mind, Daniel had shown up today wearing his service pistol holstered at his side.

Jen had frowned, but she had not objected.

Out on the water, rules were more basic.

It was deceptive too – because it didn't take long to get there – you could get lost less than a mile from one of the biggest cities on the southeast coast, and they would flat never find you.

It wasn't like the moldering corpses that they found floating in the Hudson River – the swamp left no remains.

It utterly absorbed you. *Devoured* you.

Daniel remembered a jet liner that crashed into the Everglades, back in 1992 – a hundred and five passengers, plus crew – no survivors... and no bodies.

Despite weeks of recovery efforts, all that was ever found was scraps. Bits. A jaw bone, a single tooth – a tear of torn flesh on the fuselage – victims identified by DNA.

Critters got 'em. One hundred and ten dead, total – all gone. Just part of the swamp now.

By the time the rescue crew had arrived, the crash site had been picked clean.

Daniel couldn't help wondering what it might have looked like... during.

He couldn't get the image out of his mind.

And they still had no idea what might yet be waiting within the cabin up around the bend.

CHAPTER 2

'Ranger' Daniel Reid, although chaffing in the first withering frost of his late-forties, was solid and tempered by a lifetime wrestling with the outdoors – he was a fixture on the Everglades, and long before he'd become a park manager, he'd lived on the water.

What he really liked was boating – a lot of fishing, LOTS of sailing. And there just wasn't anything more fun than those air-boats.

The creepy-crawlies, as far as Daniel was concerned, were just part of the playground – not generally anything he feared, so much as learned to watch-out for.

That did not, however, mean that he had any particular affection for them – no more than you would for a hive of yellow jackets – except as a kid growing up on the 'glades, that was more like cottonmouths or water moccasins.

And that was all a LOT worse, these days.

It had changed Daniel's mind about a lot of things. He remembered how he had been all for it when conservationists had enacted protections for alligators – it was just the sort of general free-floating-association-opinion shared by anyone who'd heard a slogan repeated often enough – but perhaps it was not a view as widely-held retrospectively, after the big reptiles bounced back much more quickly than experts anticipated, becoming a very formidable pest.

And it certainly was not an opinion held by anyone who had watched his teenaged friend's arm bitten off by an alligator at the local swimming hole.

Daniel had been the one who had pulled him to the beach – a tow-head kid named Casey, who had taken a swim across the canal on a dare. Daniel had been training to be a paramedic at the time – he'd already taken his first few months of courses, and he knew enough to bind Casey's arm and save his life.

It had been a near-thing, though. And Daniel recalled clearly, before the life-flight helicopter had arrived, several more gators – likely including the original attacker – began to encroach as he administered first-aid only a few feet up the beach.

Police shot eight gators that night. Inside one of them, they found Casey's missing arm.

Daniel remembered Casey describing the jaws crushing down.

4

"The strength of it. It was like something mechanical."

After that night, Daniel had shifted his focus to wildlife management – and perhaps looked at his job differently than the conservation-minded activists that populated his field – rather than protect the wildlife, he was more about protecting people *from* it.

The Everglades were not like they used to be. Far beyond the ecological damage created by Florida's early zoning and construction – draining vast expanses of the wetlands, literally into the cities... and all the swamp critters with it – the modern ecosystem had now been devastated by invasive species.

These days, besides the traditional swamp vipers and gators that were now showing up in people's bathtubs, you had a whole cadre of nasty new critters. The Everglades were becoming a melting pot of some of the most dangerous species on Earth.

Cobras, pythons, mambas, venomous Nile monitors – there were mean-as-hell, turbo-powered tegu lizards, that could tear a house-cat into confetti in ten-seconds or less, and leave nothing behind but the paws.

A hell of a lot nastier than yellow-jackets.

And of course, Jen loved them all.

Near as Daniel could tell, the scarier the better – she had, at various times, kept both vipers and pythons as pets. Daniel never understood the attraction – she even seemed to like yellow-jackets.

And now she worked at a croc park.

Daniel shook his head. That HAD to be the reason she was still single.

Jen was nine years his junior – although his own deceptively boyish-face made them look about the same age – something that, as it turned out, she was a bit self-conscious about.

It was absolutely unnecessary, in Daniel's humble opinion – she was lithe, but shapely, with a face that absorbed the first shadows of age like water on the sand – with ever-so-slightly pale blue eyes.

But he'd discovered that sore-spot once – *boy*, did he – just last year, after her thirty-ninth birthday, when he'd made the offhand remark that "she would be the type who would look good with white hair."

With an expression that would have turned the gorgon to stone, Jen had stood bolt-upright, done an about-face, and stalked away from the table where they were having lunch – and then had not spoken to him for two days, despite his repeated efforts to apologize.

Daniel had actually been quite surprised, and had felt bad – there hadn't been the slightest intent to insult, and it had never even occurred to him that she, of all people, would be insecure in her looks.

She hadn't mentioned it since, and seemed to have gotten over it – but HE sure hadn't brought it up.

Of course, that was not the only unspoken stricture in their relationship.

For example, while they had been good friends for over ten years, both of them knew their friendship was contingent upon maintaining the gentle fiction that he didn't find her attractive, while she couldn't see him for sour-apples.

They had both known it from the moment they met – the first eye-contact. It was a moment of pure communication, so self-evident, that neither of them had ever even brought it up.

Daniel had also learned how to be careful. Yesterday morning, for instance, he'd been helping her move a big ol' gator off someone's lawn, and had effortlessly and completely ignored the way her supple, tanned muscles flexed like a gymnast as she moved – and when they worked together, he was absolutely conscious that every face-to-face exchange was either directly in her eyes, or directly away. And he was *extremely* careful not to turn and check out her rear should they pass in the hall.

That last one was a tough reflex, by the way.

But most days, the pretense wasn't *too* hard – she was bright and engaging enough to make you forget how good she looked in jeans – another one of those compliments he'd learned not to give her.

The funny thing was, he and a couple of crocodiles were the only ones that ever got to really *see* that personality. Her public demeanor was a bit aloof – it was only in the tight circle of her comfort zone – surrounded by dangerous, fanged, often-venomous, swamp-creatures – that her chill wore off – when she was fully engaged in her cause.

And just like Wesley, who she worked for, and revered as a mentor and a father-figure, she was a dedicated eco-warrior – with a particular emphasis on the Everglades.

She took it personally that the 'glades had suffered in recent years – Indigenous species were being devastated, and Jen's heart bled for every one. And there was continued damage done every day.

For one thing, there was poaching – illicit hunting was enough to wipe out whole species. But poaching itself was only part of the black market.

And *there* was one of the real problems – the illegal trade. Besides what it stripped from the environment, there was also what the black-market kicked back, by bringing in exotic species from all over the world.

Reptiles were a particular hot-commodity in Florida – the climate suited them and they were popular as pets.

6

Which, as Daniel had often said, did not make them 'good' pets. Even legally-owned herps were often cared-for with ridiculous recklessness – everything from vipers and cobras being allowed to run around loose within a single small apartment (he'd seen it), to pythons being kept in flimsy cages, just outside children's bedrooms.

But the black-market was where it really became dangerous – mostly because of the crazy risks people took not to get caught. Daniel had heard of one midnight exchange – done just like a drug deal out on an old country road in the middle of the night – where some idiot had actually tried to deliver a black mamba to a buyer, with the snake stashed in a simple pillow-case.

Daniel couldn't help but shake his head at that sort of thing. A BLACK MAMBA, for crying out loud – highly aggressive, perhaps the fastest-acting venom of any snake on Earth – one-hundred percent fatal without treatment.

The way Daniel heard it, they had been hard-put to save the guy's life so he could face charges.

Such incidents caused some to make the argument that outlawing 'hot herps' only forced people underground.

Daniel, however, didn't see that as the issue – while the black-market was a problem, those few cases could not explain the proliferation of so many invading species. In point of fact, the real detonation point of the introduced-species invasion was not just from the *legal* trade, but the actual government warehouse where all exotic imports were stored.

Ironically, it was Mother Nature herself that kicked over the apple-cart. Hurricane Andrew blew through Florida, wiping out the storage facility, spilling hundreds of exotics out into the surrounding countryside.

That was how they got there in numbers. That was how they gained their foothold.

Pythons were among the most famous invaders – Burmese and African rocks – both big, dangerous species, that promptly went about devouring the endangered indigenous fauna – competing with, and even eating, the native alligators.

Likewise, Nile monitor lizards ran rampant – decimating local birds and small mammals – and took a nasty toll on pets and small livestock. Jen herself had reported her neighbor's chickens had been being raided for months by what they thought was a coyote until their trap turned up a hissing monitor.

And while Jen's interest might have been just such scary critters, she saw the damage to the ecology, and was highly concerned that these destructive new species might be impossible to eradicate.

Daniel knew she saw Gator Glades as a citadel against all that – she took her job there seriously, and despite her civilian status, spoke in Daniel's presence with the presumed authority of a full equal.

For his part, Daniel never argued the point – in fact, he shared her concern – because all indications were it was a battle they were losing.

The problem was that the 'glades were practically designed as a preserve – the invasive animals didn't just survive, they *thrived* – and in many cases, began to breed.

That included some very undesirables.

He wasn't sure they were *all* breeding, but there *were* cobras out there. They had also found a few 'retics' – reticulated pythons – largest and most aggressive of the constrictors – the culprit in most real-life cases of humans being not just killed but EATEN by giant snakes.

There was a gardener who was bitten and nearly killed by a green mamba while trimming trees in a suburban backyard, less than a mile from the preserve.

And unfortunately, the latest addition to the list of unwelcome and destructive aliens was a whole phase-shift worse.

Snakes could be dangerous, but mostly avoided humans. Lizards were mean, but they were small. Even the alligators – the one local beast that seemed to thrive in the new ecosystem – were mostly small-game hunters – and rather placid and lazy by nature.

Crocodiles were something different.

Two people had been killed by large crocs within the last month.

And the one they had caught had a man's arm inside it.

CHAPTER 3

The first victim had been a little girl in a canoe – eleven years old – just paddling around out in front of her own house, which lay along one of the series of interlocking canals – and she had been snatched right over the side. The second was a fisherman, grabbed out of a boat tied to a public dock.

Daniel had been part of the search crew that had found the little girl.

In areas of high-croc predation, locals said the part you always found was the victim's head – torn loose as the croc twisted and rolled – lacking the ability to chew, they tore the body into pieces that they could swallow. The head would simply be shaken off and tossed aside.

What was left of that little girl was not a sight Daniel would ever care to see again.

The local authorities had authorized a limited hunt on the 'glades – and in order to avoid a wholesale slaughter of local fauna, Wesley had also offered up a substantial reward for the beast alive.

In the following two weeks, something broke four of their traps.

Then the fisherman had been taken – this time in even bolder fashion. The man had been sitting, leaning back against the railing of a much larger boat – docked on a public pier in a high-traffic area – and he had been snatched over the rail from nearly ten feet.

The incident had actually been caught on the dock's security camera, and it clearly showed a big croc – first raising its head clear of the water, then coiling, taking aim, before launching nearly its entire body length, up to the base of its tail, clear of the water, grabbing the man and disappearing.

The audio had caught the startled exclamation of one of his boat-mates: 'What the FUCK!?"

Crocs had been becoming more of a problem in Florida in recent years. The indigenous species, once almost completely hunted out of the region, was making a comeback – and while not yet approaching the numbers of its gator cousins, the American crocodile – *Crocodylus acutus* – could get big. In fact, the second-largest croc skull in the world was an outsized *C. acutus*.

And when one of their traps had finally borne fruit, the croc they caught was certainly big – it had not yet been rigorously measured, but Daniel put it at a good fifteen, maybe sixteen feet.

But while that was certainly notable – certainly a record croc ever caught in Florida – its size was not the most worrisome thing. Nor was it the fact that it had coughed up a human arm.

First off, this wasn't an American crocodile.

In fact, it looked like a Saltie – and was most probably a hybrid.

The salt-water crocodile – *C. porosus* – was the largest and most aggressive croc – the most aggressive predator *period* – in the world.

That was not even considering what it might have hybridized with.

Then there was the second-most worrisome thing.

The arm it had coughed up had not belonged to the man taken from the fishing boat.

Among the myriad questions THAT raised, first and foremost was – did that mean there was another big croc out there?

And if the one they caught was a hybrid, what else might be waiting out there?

These days you couldn't be sure – the local ecosystem had been corrupted to the point of a mad-science project.

Besides the boom in the rather mild-mannered American crocs, just last year they had discovered a small batch of 'Nileys' – Nile crocodiles – *C. niloticus* – a hotly contested second to the Saltie in pure aggression – living deep in the Everglades' most protected areas.

Hopefully, these rather small individuals had simply been released pets – the canals were a dumping ground to hide evidence from the black-market highway – but they *were* females of breeding age. And while they didn't *think* they had been there long... they *could* have been.

Daniel knew the layman might not understand the concern – the Everglades had always had 'gators, after all.

But there was a BIG difference. And it went far beyond superficial differences like the broader jaw – although that was indicative of the true separation between the species – a form-fits-function adaptation.

A crocodile was a leaner, more athletic animal – and *much* more adapted for active predation, particularly of large prey.

Alligators were more like big, lazy frogs – mud-rooters – and while they were not to be underestimated – they could be snappy and territorial, and Daniel wouldn't have wanted to be in the water with a big one – the difference was night and day.

There was a unique consistency among those that lived or worked with or around crocodiles – from conservationist, to fisherman, to big-game hunter: NEVER turn your back on a croc.

They were purely instinctive, opportunistic predators, and if they saw food, they would try and get it – even if it was you. Captivity made no difference – they got *used* to you, which could be deceptive, but they never got tame.

Jen had told Daniel about a Niley she'd helped move during her early days at Gator Glades – only seven-feet long, maybe sixty pounds, and they had five people helping.

"That croc jumped up and grabbed one of the guys by the hand – just as quick as a whip – and started flopping into a death-roll. Broke his arm above the elbow on the first turn – damn near tore it off on the second – and WOULD have, if the guy hadn't flipped over on his side with the third roll."

She grimaced, seeing the memory.

"That all happened before any one of the rest of us could throw ourselves on top of a sixty-pound animal."

Daniel remembered hearing the story at the time – it had been before his days at the park department but the incident had made news.

"We got the guy on a truck," Jen continued. "Sent him off to the hospital – he was sitting in the back, holding his own arm across his chest – dangling by the muscle and meat."

And there was another image Daniel had kept with him since.

His hastily-scarfed breakfast of coffee and sausage-muffin tossed disagreeably in his stomach.

Truth to tell, he didn't need Jen to tell him. He'd done his research after the first Nileys were found – and the literature on the subject was not subtle. It was not short, either. When he had pulled the news reports of Jen's story on-line, 'croc attacks keeper', produced LOTS of results.

Among them, there had been a Nile croc in a Taiwanese zoo that had bit its keeper's hand off – on film. The gory incident had gone viral, with close-ups of the severed limb still locked in the big croc's jaws, as they tried to retrieve it with a long net.

They had actually managed to stitch the hand back on – fortunately a fairly clean rip – chomped rather than twisted and torn. But Daniel would still bet the fine tuning in the guy's fingers wasn't what it used to be.

Other incidents abounded – enough that many of the gorier images had been done up as tasteless memes.

Wesley was apparently aware – which was why when they went out after that patch of Nileys, he had insisted they bring along an expert.

"Or at least," Wesley had told Daniel, "a professional."

That much, at least, Daniel would allow.

The 'expert' in question was known locally as Quinton 'Crocodile' Marvin – and there was rumor that this was not his real name. Further rumor suggested he was a croc poacher from days long past – old, and wire-tough, with a heavy Australian lilt, although he also claimed to have worked for many years in Africa. Asked where he was from, he would tell you, 'France – can't you tell by my fuckin' accent?'"

Jen had been utterly scandalized to have him along. And when Daniel had met her on the dock early that morning, she had let him know in no uncertain terms.

"Are you out of your mind, agreeing to this?!" she demanded. "I can't believe Wesley is sending him!"

Daniel had seen Jen like this once or twice, but was still taken aback – just by the sheer intensity of her ire – her eyes literally flamed – as if people like Quinton Marvin elicited a physical response – sort of like a mother bear.

'Poacher' was far more than a buzz-word, in Jen's world.

It was, however, Quinton himself that demonstrated his practical value, as he had sidled up silently behind the both of them, stepping in on their conversation amiably, and startling Jen to silence in mid-curse.

"I'll tell you this," he had said, as if he'd been standing there all along, "your Mr. Wesley is a rich man. And a rich man knows expertise when he sees it, and how to put it to use. So, your Mr. Wesley is obviously a very perceptive person."

Quinton considered.

"Well, at least for a lunatic who likes to live in a house full of crocs."

He had smiled, shaking Daniel's hand with a solid, fair grip, and then did likewise with Jen, who seemed torn between the urge to match his man's grip, and revulsion with touching him at all.

The three of them out on a boat together, hunting Nile crocodiles.

THAT had been a fun day.

Jen picked the fight early on – and Quinton responded with easy conversation – even fatherly advice – cranking her pique in steady notches.

For Daniel, Quinton reminded him of the old codgers his dad used to take him hunting with as a kid – the old guys who liked to yarn.

The old trapper also demonstrated an ornery streak – every so often, he would drop a little barb in Jen's direction, apparently just to wind her up and watch her go. After the first few bends in the river, when they began to see the first wildlife – including several small American crocodiles – Quinton had shaken his head in sage reproach.

"Wouldn't have seen that twenty-years ago," he commented mildly. "Everything's so bloody hands-off, these days." He tipped a confidential eye in Jen's direction. "A lotta guys with bullets would go a long way, in my humble opinion."

The Phoenix flared briefly in Jen's eyes, and her calm reply was through grinding teeth.

"Not much of a conservationist, are you?"

Quinton shrugged.

"I'm not big on the conservation of crocodiles. They're evil bastards. There's a reason people almost shot 'em out back in the day."

He glanced back at Jen kindly. "See, they're not unpredictable, honey. They're the one big predator that, if it's big enough, and you're available enough, it's going to go for you every single time."

Quinton tossed a nod back towards the diminutive reptiles trolling along the shore.

"Now your American croc – he's not so bad. They're more fishermen. But back where I come from..."

"France?" Jen interjected.

Quinton smiled broadly. "That's right," he said.

He had paused a moment, regarding Jen approvingly, even in the unerring smolder of her glare.

"Anyway," he said, "those big salties – or those Nileys in Africa – they make what you got locally look like little puppy dogs." He shook his head wonderingly. "You Americans – you got such agreeable wildlife, it's like you feel bad about it. You gotta import your monsters."

Jen had looked deliberately away, her voice not quite hushed.

"Animal AND human monsters," she muttered.

Quinton had smiled modestly. "I don't know about all that. But I can hold my own."

And as if just to scandalize her further, he had pulled out a hand-rolled cigarette that smelled like black tar and lit it up.

In the manner of someone who knew the image he cut, he settled comfortably, a grizzled old poacher posed like Captain Ahab, whistling easily through his teeth, breathing smoke that burned like tire rubber.

In the early morning mist, with the first willow-the-wisp light playing tricks with the foliage, the smoke provided the complimentary stench of brimstone.

Jen had fallen into a sullen silence.

Quinton, however, wasn't done with her.

"Nile crocs will take people right out of boats like this, you know," he said casually, as if it were a point of passing interest.

"A professional kayaker," he said, "got yanked out of his boat by a big croc down on the Nile River, not too long ago. An American fella."

Daniel had heard about this incident too – the attack had made world news. It had, in fact, been written up on one of his own kayaker magazines – he'd recognized the guy's picture.

All very horrific.

Of course, the kayak magazines didn't tell it like Quinton did that morning – like the old man around the campfire – in the dark – out on the Everglades at four-o'clock in the morning.

"That was a big ol' croc that did that," he said, nodding at Jen, exhaling a deep drag of black-tar-brimstone.

"I spent some time in Africa. Crocs are bad wherever you find them. But Nileys are the worst. Them and salties together."

He looked casually over the side at the murky water.

"The croc that got that poor fella in the kayak was an old guy – probably a fourteen-plus footer – damn big for a Niley. It snatched him right out of the boat and dragged him under. Right in full view of three other boats. It could have been any one of them."

Quinton held up his hands, in the shape of jaws, rising straight up to the surface.

"See," he said, "that's how you know, that's not just a big croc – that's an OLD croc.

"He didn't approach on the surface like they'd seen others do – those buggers they just scattered off with paddles – or if necessary, rifles.

"THIS croc had learned."

Quinton smiled, dragging deeply of black tar.

"He came from below. He knew what he was doing – knew what a kayak was. And he knew what was aboard it.

"And," he said, "he knew it well enough to have actually developed a *technique* for dealing with it."

Quinton nodded thoughtfully.

"That means... how many times before?" He shrugged. "A fourteen to sixteen-foot crocodile? Twenty, thirty years old?"

He shook his head.

"Nothing you could do. You'd never see it coming."

Jen had fallen silent, her eyes wide. Daniel realized he had been holding an in-drawn breath.

Quinton seemed unaware, still musing.

"Makes you wonder," he said. "How many people in Africa get taken just like that? Some poor fella just headed home – who isn't some famous kayaker – just out on the water because that's how he gets there.

He gets snatched, and no one ever writes it down. He's just gone and no one ever knows what happened. Because no one ever wrote down that he lived in the first place."

Quinton waggled his tarred cigarette professorially, tapping an ash overboard.

"Think about that. How many people? Hundreds for sure. Likely thousands."

The old trapper nodded thoughtfully with another deep drag of brimstone.

"And how many old crocs?" he said. "Just like that one?"

Daniel had nodded soberly. In point of fact, he had seen the statistics of croc-predation on humans. Quinton was probably correct. Ironically, where once such figures would be exaggerated, now with conservationism an existential bias in the modern scientific community – apparently extending to include apex predators – the true death toll was likely actually suppressed.

Worldwide, there were a lot of crocs out there – they proliferated in almost every tropical climate. And in many countries – often the poorest, where populations were dependent upon direct contact with the rivers – locals weren't even allowed to hunt them.

There was a man-eating croc in the Philippines – the largest ever recorded – a saltie over twenty-feet long – and because of draconian protectionist laws, forced upon the local community by decades of western activism, they weren't even allowed to hunt it – against ten years in Philippine prison. Nope – just had to leave it out there until the government got around to dealing with it – about two years.

Now Quinton's eyes narrowed and Daniel could see the sharp hunter in them.

"And how 'bout ol' Gustave?" he said. "Down in Burundi. Big ol' Niley. He's supposed to be a twenty-footer. They say he's taken three-hundred men – that he's made his living on war dead. All the killing they've done down there, they've practically overfed him."

Daniel had found stories about Gustave too. Living in a war zone, where dealing with a problem croc was a low priority, Gustave had been preying on locals for nearly fifty years – and as far as anyone knew, he was still out there.

Jen had been absorbing all this silently.

"You really hate them, don't you?" she said.

Quinton shrugged. "Can't say I hate 'em, exactly. You can't hunt 'em that long without admirin' 'em on some level. But ya can't just bypass that the animal is gonna KILL ya."

Now Jen leaned forward – the psychological pounce.

"Someone you know?" she asked.

For the first time, the good-humored facade shifted just a little, with a deeper drag of that awful black smoke and an exasperated sigh. Yet, his voice was still patient, as if correcting a stubborn teenaged daughter.

"Honey, where ya got crocs, it's always someone you know. That's how guys like me get started. You got a problem, you just mosey down and take a look. See what we can do about it."

He knocked on the wooden rail of the boat. "That's what we're doing right now."

Daniel maintained a discreet silence.

Although he wouldn't dare say so, he found himself agreeing – lawless miscreant or not, when you were right, you were right.

In times past, Daniel himself had repeated the old saw about living with the environment – and still he frowned at the natural human urge to overreact – say a shark bit someone, there was too often a stampede to kill every shark in the ocean.

The old survival instinct, Daniel supposed, from back when humans had to gather against other, more powerful animals.

He had once sent Jen an e-mail – a series of pictures of a Ugandan native – decked-out in western clothes, holding a cell-phone – being chased through the street by a large hippo that had suddenly just up and charged right out of the bushes. Daniel had captioned it, 'Ugandan Road Hazard'.

Jen had texted back: "Really no different than walking in traffic – every now and then one of them gets you."

The unspoken point being, lest Daniel miss the subtlety, was that people didn't get scared of cars.

But while Daniel agreed there was no need to overreact or panic simply because an accident was caused by an animal rather than a car, he would have also pointed out that being eaten by a crocodile, or bitten in half and trampled by a hippo, was *different*.

Daniel had long believed 'living with the environment' also meant acknowledging the environment was not always working FOR you, and taking steps to combat it when necessary.

The public apparently agreed – particularly after the video of the fisherman was released – the unfortunate fellow snatched over the side in full view of his friends and family – although to their credit, the city was on the case, and had already authorized Daniel's parks-team to act immediately after the first attack on the little girl. One month and four broken traps later, they had caught their culprit.

Or at least they thought they did – until they discovered the wrong arm inside it.

Now, that didn't necessarily prove another big croc was out there – after all, the fisherman's body might very well be stuffed in some underground larder as crocs are prone to do – but Daniel had reviewed the video of the attack himself. And while the animal they had caught remained unmeasured, the one in the video looked bigger.

And in the way that animals had different faces, it just didn't LOOK the same. The video was grainy, and was still being analyzed, but Daniel's naked eye saw a different beast.

It was unlikely that a croc that large – let alone two – could have grown to that size unnoticed – particularly a species with that level of inherent aggression.

That meant someone had put them there.

Which could also mean there could be more even than that.

And that was not the least reason they had to ascertain this situation right away – the public would have to be informed – quickly – that their perimeters of safe behavior might suddenly need to be dramatically altered.

Daniel had learned the difference first hand, hunting those Nileys – there had been a seven-footer, just like in Jen's story – and damned if it hadn't made a fair attempt to rip his own arm off – almost the very moment he was in range. He hadn't ever seen an American croc do that, let alone a fat gator.

As Quinton had remarked at the time, with his typically droll understatement, after that first snap of jaws had missed Daniel's outstretched hand by less than an inch, "a person raised around gators might underestimate the leaping distance of a comparably-sized croc by more than half."

But Daniel could SEE the difference too – it was in their eyes, poking above the water – the way they focused – riveted on you. They were LOOKING for you in a way he had never seen in another predator.

Then there was the way they leaped on the line – Quinton nabbed them with a three-pronged harpoon that penetrated the thick armor of the neck, attaching a length of rope by which the animal was simply hauled in by hand. Daniel had used similar methods with big gators – the trick was to get their jaws taped-up. Gators were fairly placid – after the first burst of energy, they mostly let you just reel them in. But these little Nileys... it was the difference between a trout and a marlin – it was like they weren't reptiles at all, but some souped-up turbo version.

Quinton had a nice little move – once he got them on the line, he used their own death-rolls to lasso their jaws, wrapping them good and tight before pulling them up close. Unlike gators, they still put up quite a fight until you actually got them on board.

And those had just been little guys – Daniel tried to imagine pulling the same stunt with a croc over five meters.

"That's what the traps would be for," Quinton said.

Daniel had taken the point. First-hand perspective was quite different than researching on-line – the way those teeth came at you – especially after looking at all those incidents worldwide – a woman in Africa, doing the wash – a child in an Australian suburb – it made no difference – it was the same wherever there were crocs.

The Everglades had actually been fortunate – even before human hunters, the indigenous American crocodile had traditionally been a bit of a scattered presence – *C. acutus* was a very tropical animal – and besides being a somewhat more mild-mannered example of its genus, they tended to proliferate further south.

Where crocodiles were a REAL problem were areas like Africa, Australia, and Indonesia – environments where herds of large mammals routinely ventured to the water's edge – where BIG crocs waited, both conditioned and adapted to taking large prey.

Where these conditions existed, croc-predation on humans was a way of life – just like traffic.

Imagine introducing a few of THOSE animals into an area where people were used to frogs – because apparently somebody had.

CHAPTER 4

Thinking back, ever since that day, Daniel had looked at the waters around him with a new trepidation. Rounding up those Nileys had left a dip in his confidence – not to mention a new awareness of what he might be encountering in his day-to-day job.

More and more, he felt uneasy in an environment that used to be his haven.

This morning's trip through the 'glades, for example, was beginning to give him the creeps.

Not to say that by itself was anything new – every now and then, it was just like that out on the swamp. It was old instinct – the bristle of your fur – the feeling of being watched.

He'd felt that odd crawly feeling very distinctly many different times over the years – and whether it was in the mountains, the swamp, or the woods, it meant something was looking at you. Maybe hunting you.

In none of these cases had he ever actually seen what it was – cougar, bear – his dad had always laughed – 'Probably a squirrel.'

Daniel had always laughed back, conceding the point, but the truth was, he knew it wasn't any squirrel – because the sensation was real – and that tickle on your neck wasn't the sort of feeling you got when you were being watched by an unseen rodent.

And there was just something about the swamp that made that same eerie, creepy feeling worse – just speculating on what it *could* be.

You still had bears, still had cats, and now you had big gators grown fat with environmental protection.

Then there were all those pythons – every bit the ambush predator of a crocodilian – and every bit as invisible until that last moment you didn't see it.

Not to mention mambas and cobras.

And now there were crocs.

Not just crocs – at least one sixteen-foot hybrid.

It had him reconsidering that supposedly isolated, but viable population of Nileys, and all those potential eggs – four or five dozen per clutch – a species that counted on high-infant mortality. An introduced species.

For most of his life, Daniel had managed the hazards in the swamp with one simple rule – it was all about maintaining safe behavior.

That, however, was paramount upon knowing what the risks were.

Out on the 'glades, the equations were changing.

Daniel looked around at the murky river – a muddy surface that could be concealing anything – and he felt vulnerable.

Perhaps Jen was feeling the same – she sat uncharacteristically subdued and silent.

The swamp was a good place for contemplating monsters.

And it was a good degree worse when you KNEW they were there – they'd caught one just last week.

In point of fact, they still weren't sure exactly what it was they *did* catch – but it certainly *looked* like a saltie, and saltie-hybirds were often sold-to and bred in croc farms. Gator Glades pointedly avoided the practice, but there were other parks all over the world.

The croc-park hybrids tended to be salties mixed with the smallish Siamese crocodile, but as it happens, *Crocodylus* breeds quite well within its own genus.

Daniel found himself unhappily speculating on a Niley/saltie cross. Or even an American crocodile – second-biggest croc skull in the world, after all. And if two big dominant boss-crocs had been out on the water long enough to mate with the indigenous females... well, it didn't take long. How many eggs in a clutch?

DNA testing was pending, but Daniel saw no attractive option to either genetic parent. Both were large species, with individuals comparable to the largest salties – and particularly in the case of Nileys, there was that all-important aspect of temperament.

A rather nasty combination of traits – undesirable if you happened to be living around them.

Oh, yeah, another thing – these hybrids grew fast – and BIG. 'Yai', a saltie/Siamese hybrid out of Thailand, was nineteen-feet at thirty years old. And while it's not unusual for any croc raised in ideal conditions to maximize their indeterminate growth, first-generation hybridization has been known to produce abnormally large offspring – a phenomenon known as hybrid-vigor.

Those Nileys had been a small population, and Daniel was reasonably confident it had been cleaned out. But they *had* reached the intermediate growth spurt of maturity, and could have been released much smaller.

They could have been there for years.

And they had all been female – with time enough to breed.

So now you were looking at the possibility of two really large, really aggressive species hybridizing – perhaps for a while now – and most likely through some sort of deliberate human action. Did that mean there was a generation out there, growing right now?

Importing monsters indeed.

Daniel sighed. As if that was ever necessary – swamps, wherever you find them, were always rife with monsters.

Beyond just the creepy-crawlies, of which there were always plenty, the spooky atmosphere was an inspiration for voodoo witchery. and demons and spirits of all kinds.

Then there were the 'creature' monsters. Daniel had heard of a dozen different versions of Bigfoot – Boggy Creek, or the 'swamp-ape' – and they were joined by giant snakes, garfish – over in Louisiana, there was 'Black Jack Swamp' – named after a legendary monster that was sometimes thought to be a giant gator, or a catfish, or some Chimera-like mutation.

Then, of course, there was just the plain old evil-that-men-do.

While Daniel may have got into his job to manage the wilderness, it had nonetheless taught him to never underestimate his own species – even in comparison to a crocodile.

The water was a convenient dumping ground, and while full bodies were rarely recovered, Daniel was often the one charged with recovering... parts.

Like what was left of that little girl.

And when you got down to it, while what they were investigating was clearly an animal attack, every fact indicated that ultimately, there had to be a human hand responsible. Either deliberately or by accident, someone had released at least two five-meter-plus hybrids into public waterways.

Why do such a thing?

That was another thing he'd learned – they ALWAYS had a reason.

Especially when it was so easy to get away with – nothing was ever found.

Daniel found himself wondering about the fisherman that had been taken. Was he, in fact, stashed away in a croc-larder? Or perhaps in the belly of another croc?

There had been a bit of the little girl left to bury.

He wasn't sure if that was better or worse, than just being lost out there forever.

He glanced over the rail into the muddy, still-flooded waters.

And while he wouldn't say it out loud, he would have actually felt better to have Quinton Marvin's educated eye at the helm. But the old man wasn't with them today.

Quinton's reputation was as an irascible fellow on the best of days. But this would be personal.

It had, in fact, been Jen who sarcastically asked Wesley if Quinton had gotten the invite this time around.

Wesley had looked pained. At that moment, he had been standing outside the croc pen, where their newest charge had just puked out a human arm.

And while it wasn't the arm they had been looking for, fingerprint records *did* tell them who it was they *had* found.

"So," Jen had said, eyeing Wesley, challengingly. "You going to call Quinton?"

Wesley shook his head. "Let him read about this one in the paper."

As it turned out, fingerprint records had rung the cherries – a fairly extensive record of past arrests.

The arm coughed out by their captive croc belonged to one William 'Ol' Bill' O' Neil, whose cabin lay far from the canals, deep in the farthest reaches of the habitable Everglades.

Ol' Bill didn't have many friends – in fact, none that Daniel knew of.

Certainly not Quinton.

In fact, depending on what they found out there today, Quinton might wind up being a suspect himself. Him or one of his boys.

Of course, a quick look at Ol' Bill's official history gave you any number of unsettling suppositions.

Crazy people did crazy things. There was a reason Ol' Bill was a legend.

And they were going out to his place right now, to see if they could find the rest of him.

CHAPTER 5

"I knew him, you know," Jen said.

When she glanced back over her shoulder, her eyes were furtive.

"You knew Ol' Bill?" Daniel asked, incredulously.

Jen nodded. "He worked at the park back when I started. He'd been caretaker there for a long time."

Daniel shook his head. "And you're just mentioning this to me now?"

Jen shrugged. "It was over fifteen years ago."

Daniel frowned, doubtfully – that was a hell of a thing not to mention. It didn't make sense.

But maybe it did if you saw the look on Jen's face.

"He gave me the creeps," she said. "He mostly worked nights – but he never talked."

Jen had pulled her legs up next to her in her seat.

"I'd only been there about six-months when one night I caught him out feeding the crocs. We had a couple of big salties on-site. He'd gotten into the feed shed, and was tossing them frozen chickens.

"He was just out there on the edge of the pool in the dark. Looked like he'd done it a lot."

"You were the one that caught him?"

Jen nodded. "It got him fired too. But I remembered him standing there that night... just looking at me. And it was like I could just read his mind."

She shook her head, hunting for description.

"He had this... look in his eye – not afraid – but *caught*. And he just *stared* at me." Jen concealed a shudder with a deep sigh. "And I thought then, and think now, that he was considering throwing me in with those crocodiles."

Jen nodded, blinking at the memory.

"Yep. And I think if I'd have been on the other side of that door – basically, a little closer... he would have."

Daniel noted her choice of words, 'would have' – not 'would have tried'.

Jen had told him about more than one gentleman who stepped out of line – including a college quarterback whose nose she had broken, when he had tried to force her into the back of his car.

That was a story she had *told* – even with a smirk – the guy's team photo had featured two shiny black eyes with a swollen, twisted beak.

The difference was, with Ol' Bill that night, she had been afraid.

Perhaps that was something she didn't want Daniel to know.

"I went directly to the main office," Jen continued. "I called the police. And Wesley." Jen shrugged. "The cops let him go. They said it wasn't illegal for a park employee to feed the animals and that if we had rules against it, that was our problem."

"Did you tell them he was acting threateningly?"

Jen's eyes darted away – again, as if ashamed. "No. He didn't DO anything – it was just how he looked at me. What could I say? I would have just looked stupid."

Jen glanced back again. "But I think Wesley could tell. He fired him on the spot, with the police still standing there."

She shook her head. "I don't think he wanted to. Wesley said he knew Ol' Bill when he was young – he got picked on. He felt sorry for him, I guess. But something about his behavior that night... I think that convinced him."

And then in a smaller voice, "Ol Bill... right when Wesley let him go – he... *looked* at me again... and I swear I was creeped-out walking home for months."

Jen took a calming breath. "But I never saw him again."

Daniel knew the rest from the official record, which he'd reviewed after Wesley had called him.

Ol' Bill had mostly disappeared over the next few years. His name popped-up from time to time – there were a couple of visits from the rangers – mostly over things like feeding gators out on the water – illegal because it attracts them to humans.

There were also a couple of issues with codes, as he apparently had turned his property into his own private gator farm.

It was also suspected that he kept exotics on the property as well. Nothing ever came of any of it.

Jen had fallen into pensive silence. Daniel had never seen her quite like this before.

Ol' Bill had made an impression.

That incident at the park was over fifteen years ago, but Jen's hackles were up – she seemed to be psyching herself up like an assault victim about to confront an attacker.

It wasn't even like they were going to SEE the guy – not to talk to, anyway – they'd found part of him inside a crocodile.

And while it was possible they were about to see something that wasn't pretty – like, say, other pieces of him – this would hardly be the first time for that. It had been Jen herself who had supervised inducing regurgitation in their captured hybrid – Daniel remembered her holding the severed arm like a dead fish.

But that was before they knew whose arm it was.

"I never knew who he was back then," Jen said. "It was all pre-Internet, pre-social-media – secrets got kept. You couldn't just up and search someone's background on-line. And this was all years after his... problems... with Quinton Marvin and his family."

"I heard there was history there," Daniel said.

"A gator-groupie and a family of poachers?" Jen nodded. "I guess it's only natural. Except this was over a woman."

Jen glanced over her shoulder.

"It all happened out at the cabin. I don't know all the details, except that Ol' Bill had a wife, and she died that night."

Jen shrugged. "All that ever came out of it was rumors. Other stuff... blew up from time to time. But most of it all happened before I moved here. And like I said, all I knew at the time was what Wesley had told me. Which wasn't much.

"But I do know," she said, glancing back again, "that whatever runs with him and Quinton, runs deep."

"I don't know Quinton beyond that one day."

"Well, he's semi-retired, these days. Or 'going legit'." Jen held up two fingers in quote marks. "These days he contracts as a gator catcher – but he's a poacher. Always was – never thought of changing."

Daniel nodded. That had been exactly his impression.

Quinton Marvin's family had its own rumors following it, although Daniel, during his tenure as ranger, actually had little contact with them – as Jen said, Quinton was getting on in years and most of the trouble he'd gotten into locally was before Daniel would have had to deal with it.

He *had* heard about them, though. They were known as an owly bunch – deep-dwelling, hard-drinking swamp-folk.

It was an odd experience, Daniel thought, the first time you encounter people who live like animals – animal morals and animal values.

Those that went deep in the swamp, went there for reasons.

Daniel suspected men like Quinton went there to escape perceived chains of normal society.

Men like Ol' Bill, however, had gone there to be left alone... to indulge their tastes in private.

Ahead, the river was widening again.

"This is it," Jen said. "Right around this next grove."

Behind them, the sun was creeping from the east – the earliest red glow.

Red sky in the morning, Daniel thought unhappily.

The dusting of first light sent long shadows creeping over their shoulders, like spectral hands, as the ghostly touch of the wind ushered them along.

As they rounded the final bend, Daniel got his first look at Ol' Bill's cabin.

CHAPTER 6

Daniel was surprised at the size of the property – according to the deed, it was originally purchased under some sort of plantation deal – the sort with swamp-land on it.

Although mounted on stilts, the cabin itself was actually built into a land mass – split by the entwining estuaries into its own mini-island. The terrain just beyond was higher – that was the land-bridge back towards town, but likewise split off from the property by water – which, according to the map, was joined to the main road by a single-lane bridge, perhaps a mile up the road.

The property was fenced – after a fashion – even out along the water. Originally wired stakes, set up in the manner of blackberry farming, the boundary of the property was now overgrown with vines and ivy, with large trees grown into the place of posts – the result was a thick, thorny hedge, rooted right to the river bottom itself – a fort that had been grown, not built.At a glance, it was like something Robinson Crusoe would have done, if he'd shipwrecked in some lost swamp.

Daniel guessed at the actual acreage – thirty? Forty or more? Zoned when it was considered worthless swamp rather than ecological preserve, it was actually a fairly modest stretch of high-ground, surrounded by water on all sides.

Approaching from the river brought you to the rear of the cabin. The back deck was built right into the dock, which was also walled off inside the property, although a small floating platform had been attached outside the main gate.

The image was a castle wall with a moat.

A might security conscious for someone living this far out.

As he tied off their little outboard, Daniel stood and surveyed the rest of the geography. The river split the cabin from the property's primary land-mass, and again from the higher ground that led to the road.

Across from the cabin was a large reservoir – what looked like a man-made pond.

Highly illegal these days. Probably dug long since before that law existed.

And even if it hadn't, Daniel remembered the law out in these parts was Sheriff 'I'll-get-to-it-when-I-get-to-it' Barnes.

Standing up on the dock, Daniel looked over the fence out onto the pond.

Craggy backs as far as he could see.

Gators. Ol' Bill had done the paperwork to register his land a 'private gator farm' – apparently more an effort on the part of the county to collect fees than any concern over regulations.

Running along the shoreline between the river and the pond, was a row of utilitarian sheds – a boathouse built into the dock. Across the pond was what looked like a fairly large hen house. Next to that, was a smaller structure, nestled in unobtrusively behind the others.

Daniel puzzled at the odd design. While it was hand-built with the same sort of grunge-movement craftsmanship that dominated the rest, and likewise strewn with vines and swamp grime, it appeared curiously modern.

It had a solar roof-top, for one thing, looking oddly science fiction – like a spaceship crashed in a primeval swamp.

The gate to the back dock was latched, but not locked. Giving Jen a hand up, feeling their weight settle onto the floating platform, Daniel let them through onto the property.

They followed the dock where it joined the cabin. From there, the steps led up to the back porch.

And even though the morning light had yet to creep over the top of the grove that interrupted this stretch of water, the windows to the cabin above were not dark – electric blue emanated from within.

Daniel saw Jen glance down at the gun on his hip. He said nothing, simply knocking on the back door.

The sound was startlingly loud out on the water.

After a moment of responding silence, Daniel knocked again.

He exchanged a look with Jen, who shrugged.

Knocking again as he did so, Daniel pushed the door open, drawing a horrid-screech from the rusty hinges, and momentarily jacking his pulse. At his side, Jen's fingers latched painfully into his arm.

"Sorry," she said, letting go.

The blue light was brighter within.

Daniel blinked as he looked around Ol' Bill's cabin.

It was just as bizarre from the inside.

The light was from a series of terrariums and tanks – all powered by the solar panel that Daniel now saw cut into the roof – as well as a blinking computer screen – all casting the room in a spectral blue.

Like the fencing outside, modern technology seemed to have grown into the rustic setting. A blinking cell phone sat on the counter.

The cabin, however, appeared empty. A quick, cautious sweep through both back rooms revealed nothing – not even anything disturbed.

As Daniel poked around the back, he heard Jen's voice.

"Daniel, come and look at this."

He found her kneeling, looking in one of the glass terrariums – inside, reared up at her presence was an Egyptian cobra.

Daniel turned to the next tank, only to find it empty. A closer look, however, revealed a circle of leathery eggs, all carefully arranged under the sun lamp.

"He kept 'hot' herps," Jen said. "Be careful poking around."

Besides the terrariums, there were a number of what looked like refrigeration units – cases for meats – and that sort of thing – and with just a touch of trepidation – his imagination supplying images of severed limbs or some other grotesque spectacle – he pulled open the latch.

Inside, however, were rows of ampoules – chemicals – carefully, professionally labeled and separated.

Beside him, Jen tentatively turned one of the little glass vials to read the label.

"Oh, this is crazy," she said.

"He was breeding?" Daniel said.

Jen half-laughed. "I'll say. In fact, this would supply our whole park." She shook her head, talking in the full range of chemicals – some extremely toxic, most related to steroids and hormones.

"Illegal?" Daniel asked.

"No. Not really – item for item, it's the sort of thing any collector of exotics might have – particularly those that were into breeding. But not in this stock. This... this is industrial scale."

Daniel groaned, and he looked out the window after that mysterious building at the back of the compound – the one outfitted with the solar roof – steady power, just like the main house. He glanced back at the cobra in its cage.

Looking out on the main window, Daniel could now see where the front steps led from a foot bridge across the water to the high ground beyond. A small section on the opposite bank had been fenced off and a garage had been built. Daniel could see several vehicles parked inside – two-tractors, a few boat trailers – and the gutted remains of what had once been two pickup trucks.

A second bridge led over the river from the cabin to the pond.

Daniel also took note both bridges had been built high – a good seven-feet at the base, above the running water – even accounting for recent flooding – and lined with sturdy railing.

Running along the pond, a similarly-styled deck joined the series of work-sheds.

That last building in the corner, however, was hidden by the others.

Daniel sighed – any more bad news was probably waiting right out there.

He was about to let himself out the front, and go see for himself, when Jen called after him.

"Daniel. You've got to see this!"

She was sitting in front of the computer.

"Check this out," she said, and turned the monitor so he could see it.

The image on the screen was a crocodile – a big one. You could tell because the foot-bridge in the back of the frame, providing scale, was the one Daniel had just been looking at.

"And look at this one." Jen mouse-clicked to a video – a very large croc, with a scraggly figure – presumably Ol' Bill himself in younger days – feeding him whole chickens – the big croc coming right up on the bank, and snatching it out of his hand.

Daniel frowned – it took a moment to fully appreciate what he was seeing – this was not the gator-pond.

Ol' Bill had been raising this croc on the main river – fenced off, yes, but that wouldn't stop a pet dog. Both gators and crocs were known to dig.

Daniel remembered the one time Ol' Bill's name had passed his desk. It had been before he'd become department head, and had spent most of his time in the field – 'animal rescue' – which basically meant he was the guy the county sent over if you had a gator in your bathtub or a python in your backyard – but his office had received reports about gators escaping from a private residence.

Daniel had only caught passing notice at the time, but he had reviewed the incident over the past week. According to the report, the acting park head had called the local sheriff – which Daniel assumed would still have been Barnes – and the response written on the official form said, verbatim: "He's just keeping gators. It doesn't matter if they get out. They live in the swamp. He lives in the swamp."

While that had not addressed the possibility that gators might not be ALL Ol' Bill kept stocked in his little pond, it had, nevertheless, apparently been sufficient, as the matter had not been pursued.

"Can you get a closer look at that croc?" Daniel asked. "Or better yet, can you find any images with TWO of them?"

Jen zoomed in on a big croc sunning itself – pretty high-resolution – Ol' Bill had invested in his tech.

It looked like a big saltie – probably a hybrid. Just like the one they had caught.

"Same one?" Jen asked.

Daniel shrugged, doubtfully. "Hard to tell. Our croc is bigger. But I'd say that's a pretty old image. How'd you access this stuff anyway?"

"It wasn't exactly hidden. It's a slideshow program. People usually put up pictures of their kids – like a screen-saver."

She clicked over to the desktop, searching through some of the other files, and then pulling up the Internet Explorer.

"Ohhh dear," Jen said. "Look at this."

A series of sites. Herp blogs, breeding pages – and gosh, wasn't it amazing what you could just order on-line? Daniel glanced at the terrarium--slash-incubators stacked along the wall.

A croc as large as the one in that picture, even allowing for hybrid-vigor, would have to be at least fifteen or twenty years old. Had Ol' Bill kept it out here all along? Bred from imported eggs?

Or he could have snatched a few eggs – or even a baby croc – from the croc-park? He'd apparently been caretaker for years. At this point, it seemed ridiculous to think he *hadn't* been pilfering.

The croc or the egg? Which came first?

"Another thing," Daniel said, "who took these pictures?"

Jen frowned. Some of the videos looked like they'd been filmed from a tripod, but several still frames – mostly the ones where Ol' Bill looked younger – the old ones – seemed to have been taken by a second party.

"Well," she said, "at one time, he had a wife..."

Daniel shook his head as Jen continued clicking through images.

"He's being pretty casual with that croc," he said.

"It happens," Jen said. "Even among experienced handlers. Crocs can lull you. But you can't forget what they are. The ones we've got at the park – they watch your every move. You can be in their cage every day for ten years – you can even get in their striking range. But it's that one split-second that they see your eyes turn away..."

She smacked her hands together.

"I'm guessing that's what happened here," she said. "He raised this thing for thirty years – probably started to trust it. And then one day it ate him."

Jen clicked on one of the videos. "Here," she said. "Look at this."

The footage was of another feeding session, with the croc right up on the bank, snatching each whole chicken as it was held up like a dog-treat.

"See," Jen said, "it's tolerating him. That's what throws people – especially private handlers. They think it makes them tame. No. It just *knows* you – it knows you're not a threat. And it's learned to sit there and let you feed it. We do it every day at the park. They know you're throwing meat, and so they tend to focus on the meat. It doesn't mean you've made friends."

"I saw a guy swimming with a big croc," Daniel said, "when I was up surfing the web, last night. A BIG croc. Looked like a fourteen or fifteen-footer. Down in Costa Rica."

Jen rolled her eyes. "Yeah. I've seen him too. Apparently, it's a rescued animal that had been shot in the head – which could have rendered it somewhat invalid. It's also an American crocodile – not habitual man-eaters like salties or Nileys.

"And," Jen conceded, "there *are* people who can do incredible things – some people read animals very well, and just know how not to move like prey.

"Still," she said, "it's a very cavalier thing to do. A big croc might respond to positive stimuli, especially if it knows you, but the second you act like food...well, if you're that close, it's already got you."

Daniel was reminded of yet another incident – of which there seemed to be no end – where the owner of a croc farm in Africa had fallen in among his charges. Nileys. It had been over in seconds. The man's brother, who lived on the property, described the milling crocs tossing chunks of meat in the air. Hired hands recovered less than a third of a corpse.

"They call it 'selective abstraction'," Jen said. "It's common among hoarders. They're attracted to the power of a dangerous animal, and they believe that if they form a bond, the animal won't hurt them."

"You mean anthropomorphism," Daniel said.

"A specific type." Jen nodded. "It's a case where he can't perceive the animals for what they are – crocs aren't like dogs – they simply aren't capable of higher emotion. But he sees them as friends." Jen shook her head. "And he believes they see him that way back."

They both started when a woman suddenly spoke out loud behind them.

"Actually," she said, "it wasn't like that at all."

Daniel and Jen were on their feet in an instant, simultaneously remembering that they were investigating a potential crime – maybe a murder. Daniel's hand had actually fallen to the gun on his hip as they turned to the figure standing at the doorway behind them.

A young woman – a striking young woman with eldritch red hair and cat-green eyes.

She was shaking her head scornfully.

"'Selective abstraction? No. He knew EXACTLY what they were." She shrugged. "That's what he liked about them."

The young woman dropped her pack heavily, as if after a long trip.

"Yeah," she said. "He really did love those crocs."

Now she crossed her arms, eyeing the two of them.

"So," she said, "can I ask you why you're trespassing on my property?"

CHAPTER 7

"My name is Abigail. O'Neil," the woman said. "William 'Ol' Bill' O' Neil was my father."

Daniel now had a moment to take her in. He had initially thought 'young woman', but a second-glance put her at least in her mid-thirties. But her small, lithe form was hardened with a dancer's muscles – so different from Jen's long, farm-girl limbs – combined with an overdose of make-up that, on a woman past twenty-five, suggested a lifestyle where she used it.

As did those gypsy-green eyes. Daniel found himself staring.

Jen glanced at him sideways – noticing him noticing.

"So," Jen said, "Abigail. You're his daughter? Can you prove that?"

"Well, there's that picture of me on the wall behind you," Abigail responded. "And it was the county that looked me up. I've got ID in my bag."

"What can you tell us about your father?"

"I haven't seen him in seventeen years. Not since I left home."

"You were estranged?"

Abigail's green eyes narrowed.

"Obviously," she said, looking Jen deliberately up and down, appearing unimpressed. Daniel was surprised to see Jen actually bristle.

"I was notified of my father's passing two days ago," Abigail said. "So here I am."

Now she turned to Daniel, looking him directly, aggressively in the eye.

"So," she said, "who are you?"

"Actually," Daniel said, "we were the ones who found... your father's remains." He extended his hand. "My name's Daniel. I'm a park ranger."

"Ranger," Abigail repeated, taking his hand, and shaking it slowly.

"And this is Jen," Daniel said. "We're trying to find out exactly what happened here."

Abigail nodded to Jen, not letting go of Daniel's hand.

"Ranger," she repeated again. "Okay, Ranger, I think I can help you."

She brushed Jen aside and sat down in front of the computer screen, smiling as she started tapping keystrokes. "He's upgraded," she said.

After a moment, Abigail had pulled up on-line accounts from William O' Neil.

"Well," she said, "here's his e-mail."

Jen frowned. "If you're so estranged, how do you know all his codes?"

Abigail smiled thinly. "I didn't. I have a few 'particular' skills. I can also jump the change out of a parking meter."

Jen cast a raised eyebrow at Daniel, who shrugged.

"How big was the croc you caught?" Abigail asked.

"Big," Daniel said. "Maybe five meters."

Abigail smiled. "Ah. The little one. You caught Nemo. He's younger. Caesar is the big one."

Daniel and Jen exchanged looks.

"The 'big' one?" Jen repeated.

Abigail had opened another picture gallery. She tapped the screen. "There you go."

The image this time was *two* big crocs – both sunning on the bank below the footbridge – both large, but one substantially larger than the other.

Daniel also noted the low water level – that had to have been a drought year. How long since the river had been that low?

Both those crocs would have had a lot of time to grow since this picture was taken.

Abigail indicated the smaller croc. "That's Nemo."

With the two of them pictured together, Daniel could see the differences – 'Nemo' had a sharper snout, and a 'smilier' face – and the very discrepancy that Daniel had noticed from the attack footage – the armored scutes across his back were small and gnarled.

Caesar's back scutes were the large, knobbed plates that Daniel recognized from the video.

"Anyway," Abigail said, "here it is. All his financial records – bank statements – looks like he kept it all in pretty good order. And here..." she pulled up another file. "He even kept a medical log of all his animals." She pushed back, away from the desk. "And I'm guessing his credit records will give you a dozen black-market connections. Look over all you want."

Well, Daniel thought, dismally, that's two questions answered – neither of them good. They could stop wondering about introduced species.

35

And yes, there was a bigger croc out there.

"Of course," Daniel added, with a reluctant sigh, "we also have to check out what else he might have on the property."

Abigail nodded agreeably. "You mean, like in that solar-powered unit out back? Yeah, I saw that too. That's new." She smiled, heaving herself out of her chair.

She pulled a large rung of keys from a nail on the wall. And then, reaching under the easy chair, perched in front of the fireplace, she pulled out a 30.30 lever-action rifle. She cocked it once, shells loaded.

Daniel and Jen both froze, as Abigail tossed the barrel across her shoulder.

"You should see what he kept under the bed," Abigail said. She hefted the rifle. "Like you said – we don't know what's out there yet."

She opened the back door, then stepped aside. "After you."

Projecting not the slightest concern over Abigail at his back, Daniel led them down to the footbridge.

Jen glanced at the river below – its surface substantially closer to the floorboards than in the pictures.

"Caesar's gone, right?" she said. "I mean, he's out on the 'glades. We know that, right?"

Abigail shrugged.

"We know he's *been* out there. He ate someone. But crocs cover a lot of ground. He lived around here for a long time. He got *fed* around here for a long time." She turned a speculative eyebrow out over the murky river water. "He might still hang out."

Abigail smiled sweetly at Jen. "Don't get too close to the edge."

Jen looked back unhappily, keeping to the middle of the narrow bridge as they followed Daniel across to the far bank.

The reservoir was full with the recent rains, and as Daniel looked out on the surface, the craggy backs began to drift in their direction. It had likely been a while since they'd been fed.

He glanced back at the two women behind him. "Be careful," he said.

Like the cabin itself, the sheds were mounted on the landmass, but propped up on stilts. The boat garage opened up on both sides, onto the higher ground beyond, but they were all joined along the back by the decking that led over the reservoir.

Just beyond the railing, the gators followed them as they walked.

And mixed among the broad duck-like gator snouts, Daniel spotted the narrow, snaggle-toothed jaws of several small crocs. He couldn't tell what kind – Nileys, salties, maybe even American crocs.

No large ones though.

The solar-capped structure at the rear of the compound was larger than it had looked from the house – it was wide and flat like a greenhouse. In fact, it reminded Daniel of pot-grow-operations he'd busted – a perpetual sun lamp.

"Boy," Abigail said, admiring the building, "he really has upgraded. When I was a kid, this was powered by a gas generator."

"What was he growing out here?" Jen asked doubtfully.

Abigail snorted brief laughter. "Name it," she said. "I used to have to feed the damn things. These were my daily chores. Snakes – cobras, pythons – lizards." She jangled her key-chain, hunting for a match. "But mostly crocs."

She fit the key in the lock.

"Yeah," she said, "he really loved those crocs."

Abigail pushed the door open. A motion detector within activated interior lights.

Lined in rows and along the walls, were a series of incubators and terrariums like the ones in the main cabin – but these were clearly the industrial-version. Daniel could hear the low hum of steady power.

They could only guess, however, at the former occupants, because these incubators were all empty. There were not even any eggs.

"He let them go," Abigail said.

Jen looked aghast. "He let WHAT go? What did he have out here?"

"I don't know," Abigail said. "I haven't lived here in a long time. I'm betting it was nothing nice." She shrugged dismissively. "Check his computer. He was pretty meticulous about his records."

"What kind of volume are we talking, here?" Daniel asked.

The greenhouse was uncomfortably large.

What had he been doing? Daniel wondered. Looking from a purely warehouse/business perspective, it seemed like a clearing of inventory. There were different reasons for that – among them fire sales – going out of business.

OR, Daniel thought, a settling of affairs.

Were they possibly looking at some sort of ritualized suicide – letting all of his charges out first? Maybe feeding himself to his own crocodile?

He remembered that croc-farm owner in Africa had been experiencing financial problems, and a number of acquaintances had floated the idea that maybe his plunge into the croc pool hadn't been an accident.

Jen was shaking her head. "And on top of it all, you think he deliberately let out two big crocodiles?"

"Oh, you don't understand," Abigail corrected promptly. "THEY were already out. They didn't live in the compound."

"What do you mean?"

"Once they got too big... well, he just kind of let them out. Actually, I remember him calling it a 'money-saver'. They were getting pretty expensive to feed – once a croc sails past half-a-ton, it can go through a lot of chickens. But the way my father figured it, they were crocs – they were already quite capable of feeding themselves. So he let them do just that."

Abigail smiled at Jen, who was staring in gape-mouthed outrage.

"They still showed up for snacks, of course." Abigail nodded to the footbridge. "That's why I told you to be careful."

Jen was at a loss for words. "Why would anyone DO that?"

Abigail spared her a derisive eye.

"I don't know. Why do people make furniture out of corpses? Why do people put sharpened spikes underwater in popular swimming areas? Why do people start fires? People are crazy."

"Why didn't you report any of this?" Jen demanded. "You never thought to tell anyone until now?"

Abigail's eyes narrowed, and Daniel saw the feral glint of the lifestyle that heavy make-up implied.

"I was fifteen when I left here for good. I snuck out in the middle of the night after he was passed-out drunk."

She turned to face Jen directly, the rifle still casually tossed over one shoulder, but squaring-up in obvious non-verbal body language.

Jen reflexively squared up back – and when Abigail took half-a-step forward, Daniel was prepared to intercede – but she stopped short, staring Jen in the eye.

"I used to watch for that wobble in his step," she said. "He didn't drink out in the open. I never saw him refill out of the homemade potion he used to make up. But all of a sudden, he would be loaded. And mean. He'd get... that look in his eye.

"Most nights like that, I'd just hide out on the water. Sleep in the boat."

Jen said nothing. She didn't back down either.

Daniel cleared his voice. "Listen... Abigail. If the things you've told us are true, we could really use your help."

"And it's your goddamned civic responsibility," Jen began hotly. "My God, you're probably complicit..."

"AND," Daniel said, interrupting loudly, "it seems to me that any crimes committed by your father all occurred in your presence when you were a minor." Daniel cast a meaningful look in Jen's direction.

"And that we have no interest in pursuing any liability issues on your part."

Jen grumbled something unintelligible.

"But like I told you," Daniel said, "we could really use your help."

Abigail considered. Hands on hips, she regarded Daniel appraisingly – with a brief scornful glance at Jen.

"Okay, Ranger," she said. "But I need you to help me first."

CHAPTER 8

Abigail explained she had attempted to take the flooded road, getting her truck stuck, and she had hoofed it the rest of the way to the cabin – nearly two miles.

"I was going to take one of my father's boats back to town," she said, "but if you could give me a lift? And maybe some help with my truck?"

Daniel agreed to take her with them back to town and help arrange for a tow.

"It might be a day or two, though," he said. "Especially out this far. We can set you up with a motel. If you agree to help us, I'll put it on the park department's tab."

Daniel had made a quick call to Wesley, who said he would inform Sheriff Barnes of what they had found at the cabin.

"I think you might be needing to go above Sheriff Barnes for this one, Mr. Wesley," Daniel said. "In fact, based on what I've seen, the Feds might need to be notified."

"That bad?" Wesley asked fatalistically.

"Pretty bad," Daniel replied.

Now they were headed back into town – if the Backwoods could be called a town.

Abigail had claimed the seat at the head of the boat – edging Jen out of her point spot – and rather than perched like the alert bird dog, Abigail reclined, as if sunning herself on a beach.

Banished to outboard's second bench, Jen alternated sour stares between Abigail and Daniel himself.

Oblivious and unconcerned, Abigail had found a small spider crawling along the railing and had picked it up, letting it run up her fingers and into the webs of tattoos that mapped her arms.

Daniel didn't recognize the symbols – he didn't know if it was voodoo, Wiccan, or just regular old swamp-witch – nor was he especially a fan of tattoos on women – particularly on the stomach or lower back – two areas of a woman's body that didn't *need* decoration, let alone street graffiti – 'Kilroy was here'.

But on Abigail... it worked. Perhaps *because* it was so trashy – yet utterly unabashed – as tattoos went, it was elegant, professional work, and he couldn't help notice the artful designs.

And Jen couldn't help noticing him notice.

Prominent among the 'artful designs', adorning Abigail's arms and back, were intricate spider-images. The tiny living arachnid crawling along her skin was almost camouflaged.

"So," Jen said. "You like spiders, do you?"

Abigail glanced deignfully over her shoulder.

"It's my spirit animal," she said.

"What is that?" Jen asked. "Wiccan?"

Abigail shook her head. "Too formal. Call it 'pagan'."

"'Pagan'."

"Or better yet," Abigail said, "let's call it 'unaffiliated'." She shrugged dismissively. "It's really more a style than a religion. It's something I picked up from my mother."

Abigail lowered her hand, letting the little spider scurry under the floorboards.

"But we're on a hunt," she said. "And a spider is a good sign."

"You mean like good luck?"

"More like a state of mind. A spider as your animal spirit-guide means you have an affinity with acts of creation that are both intricate as well as strong – like a spider's web."

"A trap," Daniel volunteered from the back of the boat.

Abigail nodded approvingly. "Very good," she said, "You might have a little spider in you, too."

"If you say so," Daniel said agreeably. He nodded to Jen. "Say, I wonder what that makes *you*?"

The utter dead response and cold stare shut him right up.

Jen spared Daniel another moment's glare before turning back to Abigail, who appeared both pleased and amused.

"You left home at fifteen," Jen said. "What have you been doing since?"

Abigail's green-eyes were startlingly dark – like a shadow under deep water – and her seemingly soft, aesthetic features were as chiseled as hard granite. Those dark eyes turned on Jen with a knowing directness that actually caused her to blink reflexively away – Jen glanced back at Daniel self-consciously.

"I did whatever I had to do," Abigail said.

Jen turned away, muttering – perhaps intending to be imperceptible – perhaps not, "I've got a good idea what that means."

Daniel raised his brows – that was cattiness he'd never seen in her before.

Jen, for her part, was utterly aware of herself, but found she somehow couldn't help it.

This woman's threat to her was a subliminal signal – something beyond that crawly feeling in the woods – something that bizarrely resembled jealousy.

Daniel was HER pining pet, Goddammit!

It wasn't as if Jen hadn't long known perfectly well his feelings for her – she had known it the same second he did. And just like Daniel himself, she was very careful to keep everything strictly and officially platonic.

Oh, she found him likable, sure – even handsome, albeit in a 'brotherly' way. And lest there had been any confusion, she had made that very comment to him, in deliberately casual fashion, on more than one occasion.

"'Brotherly'," he had repeated back, nodding musingly, with a marked absence of enthusiasm.

There had never really been any point in discussing it further – easy enough to just perpetuate the gentle fiction.

Jen HAD, on the other hand, been reamed on the subject by her younger sister – Sally, divorced twice, two kids, and living quite comfortably on alimony, thank you – who ALSO had a long-standing crush on Daniel – had accused her of stringing the poor guy along.

"In case of emergency," Sally had said, "break glass."

To be fair, Jen's own attempts at relationships had left her skittish. Perhaps there was something intimidating about a girl who wrestled alligators for a living, but Jen had avoided a lot of the attention her looks might have otherwise attracted.

Ironically, perhaps inherent in her own femininity, she found that sort of masculine insecurity off-putting – in turn, causing her to project an involuntary contempt that shriveled the egos of the alpha-males that were prone to pursue her in the first place.

So, she had put up her own defenses, and now she was coming up on the wrong side of forty.

And not to put too fine a point on it, but Jen was considering 'breaking the glass'.

She stole a glance back at Daniel as he guided them carefully and professionally through the still-flooded waters.

He had no idea of the image he cast – amiable, actively able-bodied – he was only 'brotherly' once you got to know him. Jen had taken him out bar-hopping and had seen women practically fall over themselves to get his attention – with Daniel apparently utterly oblivious, as if it hadn't even occurred to him that he might draw their eye.

Jen wasn't certain in her own mind when she had started looking at him again – it was a remarkably long period before she got over the simple presumption of that first five-second snap-judgment the day they had met – to even recognize her own feelings enough to actually consider it.

Ironically, it was also the first time *she* had considered that *he* might give up just a few steps short of the finish line.

And now Jen found herself wanting to just reach out and poke a couple of fingers into both of Abigail's pretty green eyes.

Abigail smiled deliberately past her at Daniel, who glanced uncomfortably between the two of them.

The first bend of civilization appeared as they rounded the corner into the public dock at the Backwoods. Twenty-yards beyond, at the end of the dock was the local bar. Next door was the fisherman's shack motel. Across the street was the City Hall and the jail. Clear on the other side of town – but still not outside of a rock's-throw – was the general store – groceries – tackle – ammo. Lotsa booze.

Daniel guided them into the dock, steadying the boat, hopping onto the pier and tying them off. He extended his hand in his old-style chivalrous, pretentiously-male way, and Abigail took it daintily, practically fanning her face as he helped her out of the boat. He reached a hand for Jen, but caught the look in her eye and thought better.

"Well," he said, indicating the wilted-looking motel, "that's where we are. Jen and I are already checked in. Let's get you a room."

Daniel reached into his pocket, and handed Jen her room key.

"You go ahead. I'm going to get Abigail set up."

Jen took the key too slowly, looking him in the eye. "You do that," she said.

Daniel frowned uncertainly, but tossed Abigail's pack over one shoulder – again, Jen noted, the chivalrous male.

She watched after them as he led the little swamp-bitch to her lodging.

CHAPTER 9

Daniel spent five minutes checking Abigail in and then carried her bags to her room – stopping short at her front door. Abigail smiled knowingly as Daniel handed over her bag.

"Good night, Ranger," she said, her eyes lingering as she closed the door.

Daniel found himself speculating as he headed back to his own room.

As it turned out, Daniel also once had a brief aside with Jen's sister, Sally – who Daniel remembered as a half-cocked pistol, Jen occasionally brought along on the odd cocktail nights – and once in her cups, Sally was prone to hold forth.

According to Sally, he and Jen were both surrogates for each other – filling a psychological need at a safe distance.

Sally had nodded off towards her sister, as Jen loaded up a tray of drinks at the bar.

"It's ironic," she said, "for a woman who wrestles crocodiles, she's very much a chickenshit." Sally had turned and looked at Daniel meaningfully. "BOTH of you are."

For Daniel's part, he thought Sally was wrong – the problem was that first thirty seconds – that one moment, when his heart had broken just a little bit – the immediate-imposed distance – as close to forever as infinity would allow.

See, *he* had known something in those first thirty seconds, too – he knew she was perfect – and every moment he'd known her since, had confirmed that completely and utterly.

All but for that first thirty-seconds.

The 'brotherly' thing. The truth was, he had gotten that a lot in his day – Jen was hardly the first.

Truth was, he really wasn't holding out for her at all. It was more like after he met her, he just... gave up. She had set a standard in his heart – at the very moment he realized it was forever out of reach.

That implacable reality evoked every teenaged heartache he'd ever had.

The truth was, he was getting older and he just didn't want to go through it all again.

So why, today, did he find himself looking back over his shoulder after a tattooed swamp-nymph?

He sighed. Easy enough answer there. Big dumb male.

Preoccupied, he nearly walked right into Jen, who was standing outside her room, waiting for him, arms crossed.

"Something on your mind?" she asked accusingly.

"What?"

"Don't 'what' me. That wasn't exactly subtle."

"I just checked her into her room," Daniel said. "That's all. Why? What's the big deal?"

He was surprised to find himself defensive. Could it be he felt guilty?

Jen's scrutinizing eye narrowed. "No reason," she said. "I just called Wesley and asked if he knew anything about Ol' Bill having a daughter."

"And?"

"He said he didn't know all the details, but she apparently left home right before I started working at the park. Wesley thinks that's why he was acting so creepy that night."

"So?" Daniel said. "That' fits what she told us."

"She doesn't seem sketchy to you?"

"Very. But no worse than Quinton Marvin."

Jen frowned. "I wasn't exactly happy about *that* either."

"Neither was I, but your boss sent him." Daniel threw his hands up. "Look, either she can help us or she can't. I just want to get that big croc off the water."

"That's ALL you want?" Jen asked, insinuating.

For an instant, Daniel's temper flared. "What's that supposed to mean?"

Jen noted the spark and subsided.

"Nothing," she said, and abruptly turned to her door. "Good night."

She retreated inside, leaving Daniel blinking into a slammed door. He turned away, shaking his head, his stomach an uncomfortable stew.

"Women," he muttered.

Out on the swamp, the night creatures were coming alive. This far out, bullfrogs and gators croaked like crickets. Fireflies flickered among the swamp-lights.

Daniel glanced back towards the dock – the drop-off point that led deep into the wildest part of the 'glades.

Somewhere out there, a big croc waited – a saltie-hybrid maybe six-meters long. A man-eater.

But Daniel found his mind troubled by other things.

THAT, he thought, dismally, was when this sort of work became dangerous.

And as he lay down in his room that night, staring at the ceiling, Daniel didn't sleep for a long time.

CHAPTER 10

Abigail was waiting for them at the dock in the morning, once more sitting at the bow of the boat, her rifle again slung comfortably over one shoulder.

"First stop," she said, "my cabin."

Daniel and Jen exchanged glances, before piling their gear on board, and soon they were motoring down the river. By first light, the cabin came into view.

"Why are we here?" Jen asked.

"Well," Abigail responded with affected patience, "you're after a big croc, right? You say it broke four traps." She tapped her forehead. "Seems to me the natural solution is to get a bigger trap. Surprised that didn't occur to you."

"We did catch one big croc already," Daniel pointed out.

Abigail smirked. "Trust me – Nemo wasn't the one that tore your traps apart. THAT was Caesar. You'll understand when you see him."

"A twenty-footer?" Daniel asked dubiously.

"He was pushing that big seventeen years ago," Abigail said. "He'll be bigger now. But fortunately, I have just the thing."

"A bigger cage?"

"Just follow."

Abigail led them up to the boat garage. Attached to two trailers, were a pair of iron constructs – seemingly of professional design – both stretching thirty-feet long.

"The pontoons on the sides are floats," Abigail said. "It made them easy to transport – you didn't have worry about drowning the damned thing. It's actually more of a horse-trailer than a trap."

"Why," Jen asked, "would he need a transport?"

Abigail smiled. "Well, he didn't like them getting too close to town. So he'd go round them up if they wandered astray. This made it easier."

Jen didn't answer, but shot Daniel another stern look.

"Besides that," Abigail said, "there's a familiarity factor." She rapped the bars to one of the cages. "These meant food. In fact, that's probably why you were able to lure him into any traps at all – normally an old croc like that would be wary, but Caesar was used to it." She

47

shrugged. "And when he couldn't immediately get out, he just tore it apart."

As Daniel pulled the trailers around to the river bank, Abigail retreated to the hen house, shuffling aside the milling birds that apparently had just been living wild on the property.

She came out a minute later with a mesh cage and two hens inside.

"Bait," she said, setting the clucking chickens inside the boat as Daniel hooked a tow rope to one of the cages and attached it to the stern.

"I know," Abigail said, grinning at Jen's aghast expression, "PETA wouldn't approve. But it's what he was raised on. He *will* respond."

Daniel sighed. He knew if Wesley heard about this, he would have kittens over the optics. And of course, Jen was staring darts at him.

There was, however, no arguing that Abigail wasn't absolutely right – in fact, it was possible they could reduce this hunt to something as simple as calling the big croc into its cage for feeding time.

Jen – and Wesley for that matter – would just have to disapprove.

Neither of them had been there when Daniel had pulled that little girl's head out of the weeds – with strips of neck tissue tangled in her hair.

With a tone intended to quell any potential argument – and hopefully attitude – from Jen, Daniel said, "If it gets that croc off the water, I'm fine with it."

He pushed the trap into the water. It slid in smoothly, the pontoons balancing the thirty-foot construct better than he would have given it credit.

"Okay," he said, turning to Abigail. "Lead on."

Abigail pointed. "There's a grove of trees northeast of here. We'll set the first one there."

Stepping past Jen, Abigail took her place at the head of the boat.

In the manner of one increasingly unhappy with all proceedings, Jen quietly took second seat, not looking at Daniel as he started the boat and steered them into the current.

The trap was a drag on the smallish motor – Daniel wished he had just gone ahead and bypassed regulations – while the cage was well-balanced and remarkably easy to handle, it was still going to be hairy-going – especially in the flooded areas.

This far out in the 'glades, there was very little human encroachment – in fact, Ol' Bill's cabin was an unofficial marker – beyond was open swampland. It was as far as you go if you wanted to live like a human being – or were even allowed to by law.

And as was always the case, where humans receded, the wildlife was bolder. On another day, Daniel might have actually enjoyed the trip

– birds sat there and watched you pass by, instead of flocking at the sight of you. Raccoons and critters paid you no mind.

Daniel also saw a large python sunning itself on a tree branch, resting comfortably in the morning sunbeam.

And one of the critters he spotted at the river bank was a feral pig – another highly destructive invader to the Everglades.

Daniel sighed. Erosion of the ecosystem – evidence of it everywhere.

The new normal.

"Not seeing any gators," Abigail remarked as they puttered along the channel. "That might be a good sign. If Caesar's around, he'd be chasing them off."

Daniel had actually thought the same thing. There were several ideal sunning spots that one might otherwise expect to see gators – muddy banks with lots of leafy brush for cover.

"Wait a minute," Jen said suddenly. "What's that?"

Following Jen's pointing finger, Daniel steered them towards a sandy shoal.

A mound of mud and brush had been packed together several feet up the bank.

Daniel ceded to Jen. "You're the expert," he said. "Is that a croc nest?"

"It would be a pretty big gator," Jen said. She glanced warily at the surrounding water, and camouflaging brush. "Be careful. Mamma crocs will guard nests. She's probably close."

"Closer than you think," Abigail said quietly.

She was standing in the boat, her rifle up and ready.

Lying almost invisible in the brush, not ten feet up the bank, was a ten-foot croc.

It sat there complacently – absorbing the morning sun – but cocked like a trigger if the large object in the water should venture too close.

"Well," Daniel said, "I think we know where Ol' Bill's livestock went."

You could clearly see the scutes along the neck, making it easy to identify the species.

"That's a saltie," Jen said. "The size of an adult female."

"Not a hybrid?" Daniel asked, edging the boat a bit further away from the bank.

Jen shook her head. "That nest might have four dozen eggs in it. Maybe more."

Daniel cursed under his breath. He glanced over to where Abigail kept tabs on the mother croc with her rifle, and he was tempted to tell her to simply shoot it. Protocol was that an invasive animal be captured and humanely euthanized. But it was just that sort of time-consuming restrictions that had allowed animals like this to overrun the entire area.

A moment later, the point became moot as Abigail put a bullet between the mother croc's eyes.

The big reptile kicked, actually taking several running steps towards the safety of the water before its body caught up with its brain and it rolled over on its back and lay still.

Jen had shrieked at the gunshot – Daniel wasn't certain if it was startlement or outrage.

"What the hell are you doing?" Jen demanded, and would have moved on her, but for Daniel's hand on her shoulder.

"We don't have time for this," Abigail said. "If we're setting out traps, a little croc like this will raid it, and we won't catch the big guy."

Jen shook her head. "No. This is not a search and destroy mission. Daniel, take that gun away from her."

Daniel blinked, even as Abigail's dark eyes flashed in his direction, and for a moment he wondered what might happen were he to actually reach for her.

Not that he intended to try it – especially, considering he had just finished thinking about shooting the damn thing himself.

"I think it's fine, Jen," he said quietly. "In fact, I want to tear up that nest."

Jen was incredulous. "Are you kidding me?"

"Dammit," Daniel said, losing patience. "I'm not going to have breeding salt-water crocodiles swimming around the Everglades."

"And," Abigail added mildly, "that croc was my father's property. Which makes it mine."

"Illegal property," Jen countered.

"He had a license," Daniel reminded her.

Jen glared at him. "Whose side are you on?"

"I'm not on anyone's 'side', for God's sake," Daniel said. "In case you forgot, we're talking about invasive species. People have been killed. On my authority, I'm going to allow for emergency action."

Then he turned to Abigail.

"Now you," he said, meeting those dark green eyes directly. "Next time you do something like that without word from me, I'll arrest you myself."

Abigail smiled, offering an affirmative salute. "Yes, sir, Ranger," she said.

Daniel pulled the boat over to the bank and spent ten minutes digging the nest out. Underneath the brush, he counted forty-six eggs.

He pulled the mother croc's carcass on board – it measured just over nine feet long.

Daniel wondered how many more just like this might be spread out over the 'glades – and how long could they have been there in plain sight – perhaps mixing with the American crocs – possibly interbreeding? How strong a foothold? Hybrid-vigor was all they needed.

And who knew how many breeding seasons those two saltie-hybrids had been out there competing for mating rights against their woefully over-matched American croc counterparts?

How many egg clutches?

And it was just such a gosh-darned HEALTHY environment – couldn't have asked for better – practically a preserve.

Hybrid crocs were the biggest on Earth – popular in zoos for that very reason.

How ingrained in the local gene-pool had they become?

Daniel closed his eyes – the visual was impossible not to see – giant saltie-hybirds as the next wave of invasive species.

He found it just a touch irritating that Jen seemed more concerned about the dead animal at their feet.

Jen frowned down at the dead croc, its blood leaking into the boat.

"You know," she said, "the whole point of Wesley's reward, was to get these animals alive."

Abigail's ear perked.

"Reward? That's the first I'm hearing about *that*."

"Ahhh," Jen said. "That gets your attention. Yeah, Wesley's offering cash."

"I think," Abigail said, turning her eye back to Daniel, "we need to renegotiate the terms of my service."

Daniel shook his head. "No need," he said. "If you get us our croc, I'll make sure you get your money."

Abigail smiled sweetly at Jen. "Thanks for the heads-up, honey."

Jen frowned, but this time said nothing.

She also stayed silent as Daniel smashed the eggs in the plundered nest.

Daniel ignored her – he'd been through her guilt-trips before – she had once made him get out of his car in traffic to help an injured baby duck.

Sorry, kiddo. Not today.

Daniel took a quick jpeg of the despoiled nest, as well as recording the location, before pushing them back out into the river.

Abigail directed them through the marshes, around the bends, through some of the nastiest brush Daniel had ever tried to fight his way through. In this area, the trees grew right out of the river bottom, and at flood-stage, the thorny branches were right at the river surface.

"It's a short cut," Abigail explained. "If the flooding hadn't gone down, we wouldn't be able to get through this way. We'd have to go way back up river." She pointed northwest. "My cabin's that way – as the crow flies, it's actually not that far – but above the water is brier – you can't get through by boat."

Daniel nodded. He would have hated to get caught here when the water was high – he tried to imagine the current pulling you under those branches – like a barb-wire fence over a fast moving creek – you'd get cut to ribbons.

"Where exactly are we going?" Jen asked, ducking as the low-hanging branches grabbed at her hair.

Abigail pointed.

Up ahead, the overhead foliage finally parted, letting the sun shine in, and the river opened up into a modest interior lake.

Rising almost dead-center out of the inland lagoon, was a single large tree, sprouting out of the barest hint of landmass below. Across one long, low-hanging limb, was the remains of a rope swing.

"It's still there," Abigail said. "There used to be a tire."

She stopped for a moment – poked by a childhood memory.

"Been a long time since I've been here," Abigail said softly "They called it the 'Hanging Tree."

Her face darkened.

Another childhood memory?

Daniel turned them towards the bank, looking for a spot to place the trap.

"Where to?" he asked.

Abigail indicated the tree.

"Right there," she said. "Below the swing."

Daniel veered them in that direction.

But then Abigail suddenly stood up in the boat.

"Wait," she said, pointing at the bank. "Look there."

Camouflaged among the greenery, someone had set a large croc trap.

It was well-hidden – hard to see, even though it had been turned over, upside-down, and torn apart.

Daniel brought them in closer.

"One of yours?" Abigail asked.

Daniel shook his head.

"Pull us up to the bank," she said. "Let me take a look at it."

Daniel kept an eye on the surrounding shallows as Abigail stepped out onto the beach. Jen followed her, perusing the wrecked cage.

It was a sturdier version of the traps the parks department had been setting out for the last month – perhaps an attempt to 'get a bigger cage', as Abigail had put it.

Not only had the trap door been torn askew, the cage itself had been broken side-to-side – as if whatever had been in it, had decided to punish whatever had tried to trap it – perhaps a territorial temper-tantrum.

Daniel stood in the boat, keeping an eye on the water.

"Caesar?" he asked.

Abigail nodded. "Told you."

"So who put this trap out here?" Jen asked.

Abigail sighed.

"Well," she said. "I might have some idea." She stepped back from the thrashed cage, and reached for the rifle slung across her back.

"No matter what," she said, "we're not alone out here."

And seemingly out of nowhere, a growling voice spoke out loud.

"You sure ain't!"

This was followed by the pump action of a pair of shotguns.

Another voice spoke from the brush, almost directly behind them.

"Everybody just keep your hands where we can see 'em."

Materializing from each side of the surrounding bushes, two large hominids stepped out into the open.

Daniel's pistol was holstered. He kept his hands steady.

Jen was looking around worriedly. Abigail, however, stood careless, her hands deliberately at her sides.

One of the men stepped forward, brandishing his shotgun – "He said show us your hands, lady!" – and for a moment, Daniel was ready to go for his gun.

But then the man stopped, staring.

"Oh my God," he said. "You've got to be kidding."

Abigail smiled thinly.

"Hello Nigel," she said.

CHAPTER 11

"Abigail," Nigel said. "I'll be damned. It's been a long time."

"Not long enough," Abigail returned.

Nigel smiled, showing off a pattern of missing and broken teeth. "That goes both ways, honey."

The second man sidled up behind them. "I don't know, Nigel. Looks to me like she grew up nice."

"Watch yourself, Cecil," Nigel said. "There's teeth in that pussy."

Cecil grinned. "Ain't there always." He turned an admiring eye to Jen. "And who might you be?"

Jen's eyes twitched nervously in Daniel's direction.

Daniel, standing at the back of the boat, fourteen feet out in the water, was gauging the distance. If he could make the bank, get some solid footing...

But then there came the sound of another motor, and around the corner, two more men appeared in a large outboard – also both with guns – bolt-action rifles, this time – high-caliber.

One of the men – a younger guy – stood up quickly upon seeing them.

"Abby?" he said, perking up like a puppy. "Is that you?"

Abigail spared the young man one thin eye.

"Shut up, Pete," Nigel said, nodding at the other guy in the boat. "Mathew, will you swat him?"

Mathew obliged, with a stiff palm across the head. Pete yelped.

"You guys see anything?" Nigel asked.

"Nothin'," Pete said, rubbing his head. "If that big croc's around, he's hidin'."

"Alright. Keep an eye out. I'm not trying to get eaten out here today."

He turned his attention back to where Abigail and Jen still stood at gunpoint.

Nigel was no longer brandishing, but was not lowering his shotgun, either – and his familiarity was clearly not affection.

"What might you be doing out here, Abigail?" He nodded towards the broken and twisted trap. "Don'tcha know robbing another trapper's catch is stealin'? What are ya, poachers?"

Nigel chuckled – apparently at the irony of his own joke.

54

Daniel couldn't place his accent – it was an odd drawl – kind of an elvish-Klingon, swamp-pirate jargon – but he couldn't place it.

Based on the looks of them, it could have been swamp-ape-lingo – Everglades Bigfoot. These were DEEP swamp-folk.

Then, sounding absurdly out of place among the low back-beat of cackling loons and burping bullfrogs, an electronic ring-tone played the banjo-riff from 'Deliverance.'

Daniel shook his head. Really?

Nigel pulled out his phone – a fancy-looking iPhone X – and his mud-calloused fingers looked bizarrely primitive in the small, neon glow as he tapped the screen and held it up like a speaker.

"Hey, Daddy," he said, "what's up?"

"Got a broken trap out this direction," a drawling voice responded, and Daniel immediately recognized Quinton Marvin's heavy Australian lilt – and was now able to place the more pronounced accent of his sons – it was Quinton's ostensibly pleasant roll of the tongue bent into some corrupted offshoot by decades of backwater Cajun.

At the sound of Quinton's voice, Jen put a hand over her eyes and groaned aloud.

"Yeah," Nigel answered. "This trap's torn up too." He turned in Abigail's direction. "And you'll never guess what else we found."

Nigel held up his phone, turning on the viewfinder. "Here," he said. "Take a look."

There was a long pause from the other end.

"I'll be along in a minute," Quinton said, finally. "You all just sit there tight and don't do anything stupid."

The connection beeped off.

Nigel pocketed his phone, and took a long look at Abigail. And with Quinton's last order still hanging in the air, Daniel could see all KINDS of 'anything stupid', turning in Nigel's brain.

Cecil had moseyed up a little closer behind the girls.

"Got a little time to kill," he said.

Daniel tensed. If it came to it, Cecil first. Then the two in the boat.

Nigel, Daniel figured, would be turning his gun on him, by then. But without Cecil guarding her, Abigail still had her own rifle slung over one shoulder. Daniel didn't need eye contact to know what she would do.

But Nigel patted Cecil down for the moment, turning his attention to the ruined trap.

He gave the wreckage a couple of experimental pokes before turning a meaningful eye back up at Abigail.

"That's a big croc," he said. "Tore that trap up like that." He put a hand to his chin, pondering. "Now where, oh where, might a big croc like that have come from?"

Abigail said nothing. Nigel ran his hand along one of the distorted metal bars, nodding to the other man on the bank.

"Get a shot of this, Cecil."

Nudging Jen and Abigail aside with the tip of the shotgun that still hung casually in the crook of one arm, Cecil pulled out his own phone – an iPhone 8 – putting Nigel in the frame as he panned the wrecked trap.

Daniel had been within a breath of making his move, but now he held back – his pistol against two rifles and two shotguns, while standing on a rocking boat, was not an attractive match-up, and there was no sense in making a suicide change until it was actually necessary.

The problem was the two on the boat still had him covered. If he'd been on the bank, it would have been different – he could have moved on Nigel and Cecil together – Pete and Mathew on the boat couldn't shoot without hitting them. But standing in the boat, he was effectively trapped.

Wait and watch, he decided. Right now, they seemed to be talking.

Nigel had moved to pose at both ends of the cage. Cecil snapped pictures.

"We got a little pod-cast going," Nigel explained. "We trap gators and pythons. Ol' Cecil over there wrestles 'em." He smiled proudly. "Forty-thousand followers."

Probably no black-market connections there, Daniel thought.

Nigel smiled, as if answering his thought.

"A lot of contacts with people who got money," he said, "if you've got the product."

Nigel tapped the tattered cage.

"And our sources tell us there's a lot of money for a croc like this. Especially, a man-eater – that makes it even better."

Nigel nodded out to Abigail's pontoon cage.

"That one of your daddy's jobs?" Nigel frowned. "You get that we have a problem with you setting that out here?"

Nigel turned back on her slowly now.

"You already got a lot to answer my family for, Abigail," he said.

And Daniel felt the tension tick back up a notch.

Tick-tock.

On the boat behind him, Pete apparently sensed it too. "Nigel... stop..."

Mathew didn't wait to be asked – this time a swat in the face.

"You know," Cecil volunteered, still following Nigel with his view-finder, "shots like this will be good for the site once we get that big bastard. It's good click-bait."

Cecil smiled at Jen. "That's called 'advertisin'."

He ambled in a bit closer to the girls as he spoke.

"Speaking of click-bat," Cecil said, and now he turned his camera back on Jen and Abigail, panning slowly from the legs up. Jen folded her arms self-consciously.

Abigail, however, stared back steady – a piece of meat, open and uncaring.

Nigel approved.

"Cecil's right," he said. "You did grow up nice." He tapped on the twisted bars and held up his phone again. "Here. Why don't you pose next to the cage for us – give our followers a bit of eye-candy."

Abigail's thin smile never changed. But her dark eyes had gone nearly black.

Nigel's smile widened into a grin. "Speaking of 'product'."

From the boat behind them, Pete was standing now, ready to fend off Mathew. "Come on, Nigel. Lay off."

But it was Nigel himself who shut him up this time – just his voice, cold and flat.

"I told you to shut the hell up," Nigel said. Pete sat back down docilely.

Cecil had stepped up behind Jen. "What about you honey? Feel like posing?"

His hand slipped out, cupping her rear.

Jen shrieked in outrage, slapping the hand away.

In the boat, Daniel started to move.

But it wasn't even close – Mathew had been waiting on him, and was standing, rifle aimed before Daniel could even get his hand to his hip. Mathew fired one explosive blast in the air, before leveling it with deadly intent.

"That one was for free, mister. Next time it's your head." Mathew smiled through whiskey teeth. "Don't say I never did nothin' for ya."

Then over the water, came a shouting voice.

"Holy Jesus! What the hell's happenin'!?"

At the same time, Nigel's phone barked alive with the same voice.

"Nigel you idiot! I swear I'll skin you alive!" Nigel's shotgun was up and aimed, but his face was indecisive.

Now the sound of a motor could be heard, and Quinton Marvin came into view, steering his own tiny little outboard, with another hand seated at the bow – each armed with two more rifles.

Quinton was cussing a blue streak as he motored into the cove.

Daniel could already smell the black rubber tar from his hand-rolled cigarette.

"Hold on there, boys," Quinton barked. "That's a park-ranger you've got your guns on, ya' Goddamned fool!"

Which, Daniel supposed, they should have surmised by his jacket and shirt... but he said nothing.

Nigel bowed back, and Cecil faded a few steps away from the girls. On the boat, Mathew lowered his gun.

"That's better," Quinton said. "We're all friends here."

A short snicker sounded from Abigail.

Quinton's eyes found her, briefly, before he turned formerly to Daniel, pulling his cap off politely.

"I'm sorry folks. My sincere apologies." He scowled over his shoulder. "My boys ain't got no manners."

Then he turned and looked directly at Abigail.

"But I guess you know that, don't you, Abby?" he said.

Abigail still hadn't made a move – just stared back with those strangely dark eyes – blood-pressure forcing the iris to expand – feline eyes.

"These are your boys, Quinton?" Daniel said, using his cop-voice.

Quinton tipped his hat. "Just the good-looking ones," he said. "Mathew and Cecil over there are hired hands. So's Barney, here." He tossed an ash in the direction of the man in the boat beside him.

He took another drag, this time blowing a plume in the direction of the demolished trap.

"Looks like he made short work of that one, didn't he? I've been taking a quick circle – tryin' to see if he's in the area."

Another deep drag – puffing it out like a dragon.

"How big, ya think?" he said. "Twenty-footer?"

Quinton chuckled a little, rubbing his fingers together.

"Pretty penny for that one," he said.

"So," Jen said, prodded out of her silence, "I guess you're going to kill it for some rich man's trophy room?"

Quinton looked distressed. "Oh, no, girl, you got me all wrong."

He held up his own IPhone 8 plus.

"See," he said, "these gadgets make it so much easier than the old days – this is just a list of rich bidders, all throwing money at me. And they ALL want it alive." He shook his read reassuringly. "See, girl, I'd stand to lose a lot, by bringing it in any other way."

Daniel added crossed arms to his cop's voice.

"What are you doing out here, Quinton?" he said. "I'm game management. You haven't been called on board. Specifically, YOU weren't called on board."

"Not by you," Quinton replied. "We're on to hire by whoever wants us."

"What does that mean?"

"It means we're a legitimate business. We clear out gators and pythons – or we'll even round a few up for you. And that includes crocs."

"Does Wesley know you're out here?" Jen interjected, her knee-jerk ire pushing her fear aside.

"Let's say, 'no'," Quinton said. "Officially."

He took a drag of his brimstone-tar-stick.

"In fact," he said, "let's just say, 'no' – period. But I expect him to be forgiving."

Quinton shrugged. "After all, if we get that big bugger, he'll get a fair bid."

"If you're going into unauthorized waters, you could be arrested," Daniel said – formal cop voice.

A mistake. Nigel had his own knee-jerk response. "Can't have that," he said and pumped his shotgun. Like a flock of birds, the others responded, and suddenly Daniel was looking at five separate barrels.

Quinton was standing in his boat, cussing again.

"For God's sake!" he shouted. "Will ya shack 'em up, boys? We aren't going to be shooting anyone here, today." He eyed Nigel. "Not unless I'm pelting your stupid ass. Understand?"

Nigel grumbled reluctantly.

Quinton pitched his cigarette – it seemed to fizzle like grease on swamp gas as it burnt out on the water.

The old trapper sighed.

Then he turned to Abigail – whose cold stare never wavered.

Quinton measured her with a regretful eye.

"It doesn't have to be like this between us, Abigail," he said. "The people that hated each other are all gone."

Abigail blinked once – a computer receiving contradictory data.

"Not '*all*'," she said.

There was a heartbeat of silence on that moment – one of those pivotal points where decisions determine events – the butterfly effect – where a thousand possibilities exist.

But the look in Abigail's eyes told Daniel that there was really only one. And like it or not, Quinton knew it too.

Cecil, however, was apparently more forgiving.

"Hell," he said, "I don't bear no grudges." And with that, he reached out a caressing hand up Abigail's thigh onto the curve of her shorts. But Abigail's reaction was a bit more emphatic than Jen's.

With the casual agility of a ballet dancer, Abigail turned and kicked Cecil dead in the nose, her bare-feet curling her toes back like a palm-strike.

Cecil staggered, his face exploding blood, dripping his gun, and as his hands went to his face, Abigail kicked him with practiced precision in the groin – the crack was like the sound of an experienced home-run hitter catching meat.

Cecil's face contorted into a rictus of unbelievable agony and he dropped like a stone.

Abigail yanked the rifle from her shoulder.

Nigel was bringing up his shotgun, but she already had the barrel leveled between his eyes.

"Easy, boys," Quinton said, and the others kept their guns obediently at their sides.

Nigel smiled down the barrel of Abigail's rifle.

"Nice kick," he said. "That's what seven-inch heels sliding around a pole five-hours a night will get ya, I guess."

Abigail's head cocked, her green eyes swelled obsidian black.

Quinton's voice was steady.

"That's enough of that, boy," he said.

Quinton bowed his head, and brought one knee up on the railing, looking at Abigail earnestly.

"For what it's worth, Abby," he said, "I'm awful sorry for what my boy did to you. I could say it's not the way I raised him. But I guess I did after all."

The old man shrugged regretfully. "I mean, he WAS awful mad about his brother. Not that it forgives him none."

Quinton fell silent a moment, bent over the water on one knee. And when he spoke, the regret in his voice had been replaced by real pain.

"But I dare say," he said, "what happened to him was worse."

He eyed Abigail seriously.

"Lot of rumor out on the swamp. And rumor has it, your daddy might have had something to do with it."

For the first time since Daniel had known him, Quinton's amiable manner had gone dead serious.

"Rumor has it, your daddy fed my boy to one of his goddamned crocodiles."

Abigail shrugged, her rifle still poised on Nigel – who, for his part, seemed to be wrestling with his own arms, just to keep his own weapon at his side – a dog not quite willing to jump before his master's command.

"I don't know about all that," Abigail said. "But I do know he fucked with the wrong bitch."

She smiled down the barrel at Nigel.

"Anyway," she said, "he's long-since gator-shit."

Nigel's face went dead-flat.

"Bitch," he said.

Without another word, he moved forward, raising his shotgun, his eyes set with clear purpose.

As he moved, Abigail fired.

The gunshot was an explosion that echoed for miles in the swamp.

Nigel's shotgun was blasted in half, and both pieces went spinning out of his grip. Nigel cursed, shaking his hands, turning to see Abigail ejecting the shell and levering the next one in place. She raised the barrel to his head.

But now, from his own boat, Quinton had his own rifle up.

"That's my son, ya got there, Abby," he said. "I don't have as many of those as I used to."

"Then get out of here," Abigail said, not looking over. "Or I'll kill him."

Quinton nodded. There was no question that she meant it. Threatening to shoot her back, would just make sure of it.

"Alright boys," he said. "Round her up and let's go." He nodded at Nigel. "Leave the bloody trap."

Abigail followed Nigel with her rifle as he clambered aboard Quinton's boat, helping Cecil along, who was not quite yet moving on his own power.

"If I see you out here again," Abigail said, "I'll shoot first. Just like my daddy would. Same rules apply."

Quinton paused, lighting up another hand-rolled tar-stick.

He took a deep breath as if the ghastly mix were a euphoric mist.

"I meant it," he said, "when I told you it doesn't have to be like this between us. There's no reason we can't be friends. Or at least not hate each other. I never had a problem with YOU."

Abigail never blinked.

"Maybe you should have," she said.

Quinton nodded mildly. He waved to the others. "Let's go, boys."

Within minutes, the sound of their motors were fading in the distance.

When they had gone, Daniel turned to Abigail.

"That was a hell of a good shot," he said.

Abigail slung her rifle back over her shoulder.

"Like hell," she said. "I was aiming for his head. His shotgun got in the way."

Daniel and Jen exchanged glances.

It was Jen who asked the question Daniel wouldn't have dared.

"What," she said, "did Quinton's son do to you?"

Abigail's cat-black eyes flashed at her coldly.

"I was a teenaged girl. What do you think he did?"

"And," Daniel asked quietly, "what... happened to *him*?"

Abigail shrugged. "He went missing a few weeks later. They found his overturned boat."

She shook her head, in mock regret.

"It happens that way, sometimes. Out on the swamp."

Jen cleared her voice, glancing at Daniel. "So. Just karma, I guess?"

And now Abigail smiled. And it was the creepiest smile Daniel had ever seen – like vampire teeth on a pretty face.

"I guess. He was a drunken lout. And the water doesn't suffer fools. It was bound to happen, sooner or later."

She turned, staring at the both of them challengingly.

"A few weeks too late, for all of me," she said.

Daniel and Jen sat silent, absorbing the lesson.

Abigail tossed her head dismissively.

"Anyway," she said, "I don't worry over it. Whatever it was that happened to him, the swamp's long since digested him by now. Every piece."

She pointed to the 'Hanging Tree' again.

"Come on," she said. "Let's set out our trap."

CHAPTER 12

They ended up setting out two traps – the one at the lagoon, and then a second one further up river towards the populated areas – along the route between the cabin and the first attack.

Once they'd docked up back in the Backwoods, Daniel called Wesley and reported the incident with Quinton and his boys.

"It got damned violent," Daniel said.

There was a long pause. When he finally spoke, Wesley's voice was cautious.

"It was actually this young woman – Mr. O' Neil's daughter – that took the shot?"

"In self-defense." Daniel found himself losing patience.

Wesley seemed to sense it. "I know, I know," he said. "Listen. I believe you. I'm just trying to figure out what to do about it."

"Arrest them?"

"Well," Wesley said, apologetically, "I can make a call to the local jurisdiction sheriff."

Daniel muttered a curse. That would be Sheriff Barnes.

"Great," he said. "Now I'm filled with optimism."

"I can ask the state cops to step in," Wesley said. "I can't order it – that's out of my immediate authority. But I can make some calls."

Daniel sighed in exasperation. He knew Wesley was only thinking from his own perspective – as a politician, at least part of his concern was bad publicity.

There was, however, no avoiding it this time.

"Call the state cops," he said. "Just get them up to speed. I'll go talk to Barnes, so we can say we went through proper channels."

Daniel found himself a bit chagrined, talking like a politician himself.

"I'll do what I can," Wesley promised. "But be careful out there, Daniel. I don't need to tell you – don't forget where you are."

"I won't."

Daniel hung up, and turned to find Jen standing in his doorway.

"Where's Abigail?"

Jen tossed a thumb over her shoulder in the direction of the general store.

"Polk Salad Annie said she was going to get some groceries and go to bed." Jen eyed him seriously. "Daniel, we need to talk."

"I'm headed over to the Sheriff's office," Daniel said.

Jen sighed. "Sheriff Barnes?"

Daniel nodded.

"Okay," Jen said. "Let's go."

It was the first time Daniel had actually met Barnes in person, and the first thing he thought was how you always hear how people don't look like their voices – that was not the case here.

The wry, cantankerous drawl Daniel remembered from the phone was practically a caricature face-to-face – almost a cartoon.

Barnes had been sitting in the window at his desk – tapping away at an I-phone – and Daniel could see him watching out of the corner of his eye – just like a croc – as he and Jen crossed the twenty paces to the city jail. He made no attempt to hide a disgruntled sigh as they entered his office.

"Help you folks?" Barnes ground out a hand-rolled cigarette that was every bit as foul as Quinton Marvin's black tar-stick.

The sheriff's face was uninviting, and even less so, when Daniel introduced himself.

Neither did he seem particularly happy with what Daniel was there to tell him.

"I told you I'd check out that cabin," Barnes said. "Now you got it all stirred up."

Jen blanched. "Are you kidding? We were assaulted!"

"And ol' Abigail took a shot at 'em, did she?" Barnes shook his head. "Thought we were well-rid of that one."

"Listen, Sheriff," Daniel said, "Councilman Wesley is going to be in contact with you. You need to understand – we've found evidence of potentially serious ecological damage. This jurisdiction is going to be statewide. Probably federal."

"But in the meantime," Barnes said, "you're stuck with little old me." He gestured to his office. "I don't think you understand. I'm it. And you're talking about a bunch of pretty tough customers."

"Are you saying you're afraid of them?" Jen asked.

"I'm saying only a foolish man starts a fight without knowing what he's getting into. They're all a pretty rough bunch. And they've been on the shady side of the law since their daddy showed up stateside back in the day."

"We've met their daddy," Daniel said.

"Then maybe you'll take my point," Barnes said. "Thing is, I can't arrest the whole family and all their hired hands. I also can't offer you twenty-four hour protection. You get what I'm saying?"

"They'll come after us," Daniel said.

'Probably will, anyway." Barnes shrugged. "I can arrest them after the fact. But you need to think about what's after the fact."

Jen was shaking her head. "This is crazy. Can't you even roust them for poaching? I mean their trap is still out there! You're the law, right?"

Barnes leaned back in his chair, and tapped on the wooden wall behind him.

"From here to here," he said, "what I say goes. But out on the water?" Barnes whistled through his teeth. "That's pretty much Darwin."

Now Barnes sat forward, looking at the two of them seriously.

"The fact is, I do pay attention to what goes on in my territory. My first job is to keep people safe from it. Beyond that, it's politicians – like your Mr. Wesley.

"Poaching," Barnes said dismissively, "really isn't my problem – it's not done like it used to be anyway. Leastwise, not for dead animals. These days collectors want 'em alive. Personally, I always thought that was pretty stupid if you were talking about a damn rattlesnake."

Barnes paused a moment, as if to ponder the notion – not for the first or the hundredth time – coming up flummoxed yet again.

"Anyway," he said, "these days, it's all about live-trade. That's where the black-market money is."

Barnes considered. "I suppose, lookin' on it that way, it's probably better. Black market money's always being made, but this way, no animals have to die."

"Are you saying this is the way Quinton's making his money?" Jen asked.

"I'm not saying a damn thing," Barnes responded. "But it sure would make sense, wouldn't it?"

"What about Ol' Bill?" Daniel asked.

Barnes' expression darkened. "I think that ol' boy – he might've been in it. But..."

The Sheriff faded off. Across the way, Abigail was coming out of the general store, a bag of groceries tucked in one arm. She didn't look over.

Barnes frowned as he watched her.

"There's a wild one there," he said. "You know her story don't you?"

"Just rumor," Daniel said.

"Rumor's all there is, out these parts," Barnes said. "But I can tell you on good authority that Ol' Bill ran afoul of Quinton Marvin's people on account of Abigail's mother."

Jen nodded. "I've heard something about that."

"Pretty one she was. Called her Lotus. And just like you'd figure, she had more than one fella after her. Story was, she and Quinton's oldest son, Johnny were an item. There was even a further rumor that she didn't exactly leave him for Ol' Bill by her own volition.

"In fact," Barnes continued, "the way I hear it, 'twas a while before they even knew he had her. Thought she'd just vanished in the swamp."

"By the time they figured it out," Barnes said, "she had a little girl."

Barnes glanced out to the street, but by now Abigail was gone.

"Things went south one night."

"Johnny," Daniel said, "tried to get her back?"

Barnes nodded.

"Ol' Bill kept gators. Story was there was a scuffle – Ol' Bill and Johnny – and she fell in among 'em."

"So what happened?" Jen asked. "Was anyone arrested?"

"Sure. But push comes to shove, it was basically an accident. Nobody stayed there long. Not Ol' Bill. Not Johnny." Barnes shrugged. "It was before my time."

"Course ol' Johnny," Barnes said, "he disappeared shortly thereafter. Out on the swamp. Found his boat capsized."

"Coincidence?" Daniel said.

"He was a gator poacher," Barnes replied. But he met Daniel's eye meaningfully. "Of course, people talk. And I can tell ya, things were none too good between Ol' Bill and Quinton Marvin after that. Him or none of his boys."

"Abigail," Jen said, "mentioned... an assault."

"That would have been Virgil – Quinton's second-oldest."

"And Abigail said he disappeared as well," Daniel said quietly.

"About three weeks after," Barnes nodded.

"And that didn't seem suspicious?" Jen said, incredulously.

"It did," Barnes said. "Questioned everybody. No witnesses. No bodies. That's the thing – even swamp-scum got rights."

Barnes leaned back in his chair, folding his hands across his belly.

"On the other hand," he said, "that doesn't mean I miss a few of 'em, when one or another of them goes missing now and again.

"The swamp," Barnes said, "doesn't need a motive."

CHAPTER 13

"You know," Jen said, "I'm kinda wanting to clobber that little swamp-bitch."

Her voice carried across the little tavern, and the half-dozen other patrons glanced in their direction.

Daniel made a placating motion with one hand – 'quiet down' – which kicked Jen's temper up one more notch.

"Seriously," Jen said, "are you really bringing her out again tomorrow?"

Daniel threw up his hands. "She's got traps. She's got knowledge and experience. We need her."

"After everything Barnes just told us? After what she did today? Do you realize she almost killed somebody? Not to mention what she did to that mother croc."

"Do you realize," Daniel responded – a touch more assertively than Jen was used to from him – "that she might have actually saved both our lives?"

"Or almost got us killed."

"They had guns on us, Jen." He shook his head. "They were already putting their hands on you."

Jen's temper flared again – even just at being reminded of that humiliation – let alone that he would USE it.

"I can take care of myself," Jen said hotly. "And I sure don't want my back covered by some crazy, gun-happy, straight-razor, swamp-skank."

"Jesus, Jen," Daniel said, and now his own voice raised. "Will you listen to yourself?"

Jen would not be cowed. "Will you listen to *your*self! Do you have any idea how you've been acting around her?" She leaned in close, looking him directly in the eye. "She is SO not your type."

Daniel stared back stonily. Jen could see that had stuck him – and she had already prodded his temper.

"Well," he said, "at least she doesn't seem to see me as a brother."

There was an awkward heartbeat of silence as both of them contemplated the heavier truth behind the comment – as well as the fact that he'd made it – the breaking of that gentle fiction.

For a moment, Jen wasn't sure she would rise to it.

But her own temper had been sparked. That, and perhaps something else.

"OR maybe she's just that sort of swamp-trash that it doesn't matter."

They stared across the table at each other, with real anger – perhaps for the first time since they'd known each other – saying things that were meant to hurt.

It was another one of those pivotal moments – engage, withdraw, or go for the kill – and then things would be different afterwards forever.

And during that moment that they sat silent, contemplating those options, the door to the tavern swung open heavily, crashing against the wall, letting in a gust of boisterous laughter.

"Oh no," Daniel muttered, as four beefy figures wrestled their way inside, already buzzing with whiskey fumes, still wet from the river.

Quinton's boys. And hired hands.

Nigel and Pete, with Barney and Mathew in tow – Cecil was absent – perhaps nursing his broken nose.

And naturally, Quinton – voice of reason that he was – wasn't there.

Nigel was the first one to spot them.

While the rest clambered into what was apparently their regular booth, Nigel turned, pulling off his coat, and stared directly into Daniel's eyes.

Any hope of avoiding confrontation was immediately dashed, as Nigel marched directly to their table.

He sat his hands down loudly, rattling their drinks, and stared in Daniel's face dangerously.

"You need to get out of my bar, boy."

Daniel stared back, not saying anything, and Jen actually found herself irritated. Mr. Nice-guy wasn't going to scare anybody. She wondered if he was going to agree to leave, just to avoid trouble.

"Course," Nigel said, "the lady can stay."

He reached out and put his hand on her wrist.

With the sort of casual speed that she'd seen him grab a copperhead out of someone's backyard, Daniel snatched Nigel's hand right back off her wrist. With the same snap-reflexes, he twisted the captured hand – eliciting a startled squawk from Nigel.

Behind him, Mathew and Barney were standing. Pete was pushing out of the booth, reluctantly bringing up the rear.

It might have gone further except for the bartender, who double-pumped a shotgun, eyeing Nigel meaningfully, in the manner of one who had done it before.

Daniel let Nigel's arm go – stepping back warily – just like releasing a big gator.

Nigel rubbed his arm, glaring.

The bartender tapped the butt of the shotgun once on the bar.

"Goddamnit, Nigel," he said, "even one broken glass tonight, and I'll decorate this wall with your brains."

"Fuck you, Clyde," Nigel said, but nevertheless, turned away balefully.

Daniel discreetly ushered Jen from their booth, leaving their two half-finished beers, and tossing two twenties on the bar.

"Keep the change, Clyde," Daniel said as they retreated out onto the street.

Jen, however, was waiting for him, and had no intention of letting anything go.

"We've got to talk about this, Daniel."

But Daniel had had enough.

"No," he said, "we don't. First of all, we aren't going to 'talk' until I do what you want. Second, right at this moment, I'm looking at Abigail O' Neil as our best chance to get that big croc off the water, fast, as well as assessing the full extent of what her father might have set loose out here. That makes her an asset."

And apparently because she just couldn't help herself, Jen muttered, "Yeah, I've seen her assets."

Daniel looked at her steadily.

"If you'd like, I can take you back to town," he said. "The parks department can handle things here."

Jen stared back, and while her face didn't show it, that was as close to a physical slap as she had ever taken from Daniel.

I don't need you.

And maybe even, I don't WANT you.

Without a word, without agreeing or denying, Jen turned on her heel, retreating to the hotel.

Standing in the street outside the bar, Daniel let her go.

Jen turned the corner outside her room. And just the moment he was out of sight she felt tears welling.

With a throb of frustrated anger and near physical pain, she fought them back – oh, she would be goddamned if she was going to cry here tonight – and only one brief sob escaped her – a brief choke before she bottled it all up again.

She took a moment to compose herself, and had just done so when she was grabbed from behind by two ape-like arms and a hand thrown roughly over her mouth.

Nigel's whiskey voice breathed in her ear.

"Gotcha, bitch!"

Jen was utterly astonished to find herself helpless.

She spent her days wrestling gators and crocs, yet this man curled both her hands behind her back like a little girl.

Shock bled into outrage as she began to fight – Jen had taken karate and self-defense lessons since she was a kid – to be manhandled was so foreign to her it didn't even immediately occur to her to scream.

But by then, the big calloused hand had clamped over her mouth so tightly, she couldn't even bite.

She struggled herself to sheer exhaustion in less than a minute.

"That's it, girl," Nigel whispered. "Easy now."

She shut her eyes, and suddenly felt herself jerked roughly, and thought for a moment, he had pushed against the door of her room.

But when she opened her eyes she realized it was Daniel.

He had twisted her from Nigel's grip and flung her aside.

Nigel's face contorted in anger, but Daniel had him by the wrist.

There was a momentary pause, as Daniel seemed to be waiting – was it a boy-scout move, Jen wondered? Waiting for the other guy to swing first?

A second later, she realized that was not the case – rather, he was waiting on the strike – just like catching a python. When Nigel started to swing, Daniel gave his arm a little tug, throwing off the punch and gaining control of his opponent's momentum.

Daniel would have probably been gentle with a python. With Nigel, he stepped forward and knocked him cold.

It was almost comical – the startled look on Nigel's face as he was stretched out, wide-open, and just blasted into unconsciousness.

Jen would not soon forget the loud 'crack' – like when a karate master capable of breaking a brick actually lands on a human target. Jen had read that breaking a human skull required similar striking force as breaking a coconut. The smack on the end of Daniel's knuckles was pushing that boundary.

Nigel lay stone still.

At the corner of the alley, Mathew and Barney separated from the shadows – two big beefy bruisers. A third shadow joined them as, reluctant or not, Pete dutifully followed.

"You should not have done that, boy," Mathew said, and the three of them fanned out to either side.

Mathew and Barney stepped forward, producing blades.

Daniel had left his side arm in his room, so instead pulled out his car keys, wrapping the jagged edges around his knuckles.

He actually smiled as he spoke – and his voice was low and dangerous and frightening.

"*Come on*," he said.

Jen actually felt a touch of goose-flesh. Once, in high school, she'd been alone at home with the family Labrador, and the dog had suddenly turned and started growling at the back door – not snarling, not showboating – but a low, rumbling, absolutely serious, no-shit growl – hackles raised, pointing at the back door.

There had been nothing there when she'd circled the backyard with a fire poker – likely a coyote or a raccoon – but she still remembered the cold chill at that rumbling menace coming from that teddy-bear Labrador face.

And facing three armed-thugs, Daniel sounded much more like a wolf than a friendly lab – the advancing trio actually paused.

But this time, it was no shotgun-pump that stopped it, but a blast fired straight into the air. The shot was followed by a barrel pointed right down the alley.

Sheriff Barnes was talking into his I-phone. "Yeah, Clyde. You were right. I got 'em."

A second uniformed man appeared at the alley, also with his weapon drawn, and advanced quickly.

Barney and Mathew exchanged glances, dropping their knives. Pete showed his hands.

The second cop was a young guy, who looked excited as all hell to have his gun out.

Rather than take chances, Daniel dropped his car keys.

He turned to Barnes, who was poking his foot at Nigel's unconscious body.

"I thought you worked alone," Daniel said.

"This here's Hendricks. He's part-time. I thought I'd bring him on nights for the next week or so." Barnes kicked at Nigel a final time, apparently for good measure, before giving up. "Looks like it's a good thing I did." He turned to Daniel seriously. "And it's a good thing ol' Clyde called me."

"Thank him for me," Daniel said.

Barnes nodded to where Nigel still lay motionless. "Hendricks, you wanna load that idiot up, and throw him in the cage?"

Hendricks nudged Nigel's inert form. "Should we maybe take him to the hospital?"

Barnes shrugged. "He'll be alright. Or if not, fuck him." The Sheriff pointed to Mathew and Barney. "Lock them up too," he said.

Barney started to curse, but was silenced by a quick look from Barnes. Hick-sheriff or not, Quinton's boys apparently weren't about to give him any shit.

Mathew scowled in Pete's direction. "You know you gotta bail us out," he said. "And call up your daddy."

Pete nodded, mollified, and retreated in the direction of the dock.

Barnes turned to Daniel, nodding to where Barney and Mathew were helping Hendricks carry Nigel across the street to jail.

"Anybody else you hit like that and I'd arrest you," he said.

"Pretty clear-cut self-defense," Daniel said.

"That's what I mean. Anyone else and I might have had doubt, and I'd have at least taken you overnight."

Barnes tipped a glance to Jen. "But I got a good idea of what ol' Nigel had in mind."

He regarded the both of them – a man with no patience for pretense.

"So," he said, "are you two gonna stay in town? Not to put too fine a point on it, but I'd really like to see you both gone. For everyone's sake. Sticking around is just asking for trouble."

"We've got an animal killing people," Daniel said.

"So let THEM deal with it," Barnes replied, exasperated. "What's the worst that could happen? They kill it? They make a little money catching it? Hell, it might even eat one or two of them. Win-win."

"Or," Jen said, "the idiots CAN'T catch it and it kills somebody else."

"Besides," Daniel continued, "it isn't just about the crocodile. I told you, we need to get a look at the local waterways. The ecology is at stake."

Sheriff Barnes let his breath out in a tired whistle.

"The eee-cology," he sighed. "Ol' Bill was up to dickens out there, was he?"

Barnes was shaking his head, and now the cantankerous grouch faded into the concerned elder.

It seemed genuine enough.

"Curiosity killed the cat," he said. "Really folks – if might be best to just look the other way this time."

Jen frowned, deflecting this sage wisdom skeptically.

"I think Councilman Wesley might object to that," she said.

Barnes smirked at the name. He eyed Jen meaningfully. "Lord," he said, "save me from idealistic fools."

With that, Barnes grabbed up his hat.

"Alright, folks," he said, "just remember – anything that happens, you only got yourselves to blame. It's all the same to me."

He pulled up another of those damp-looking, hand-rolled stogies – smelling like burnt gas even before it was lit. He stoked a match and breathed a plume of pure black-tar.

"That's the thing about the swamp," he said. "It doesn't even leave anything to clean up."

Barnes tipped his hat, turning back towards the jail.

"Night folks."

His fading footsteps, however, were replaced by another sound – that of two clapping hands.

Standing at the door to her room, Abigail was applauding.

"Well, well, Ranger," she said approvingly. "Way to go. I wish I'd gotten THAT punch on camera."

Her dark eyes fluttered dramatically, nodding to Jen. "You've got yourself a hero, don't you, honey?"

Jen blinked, glancing at Daniel self-consciously.

"It would," Daniel said, "probably be a good idea if everybody locked their doors tonight."

Abigail smiled broadly, looking him up and down. "Who needs doors?"

Daniel looked to make an issue of it, but Abigail raised a placating hand.

"It's okay, Ranger," she said, "I'll lock my door."

And with a last knowing wink at Jen, Abigail retreated back inside.

Daniel turned to Jen, looking reluctant.

"So," he said, "are you staying or going?"

Jen blinked – that was maybe the second-worst verbal slap he had ever given her. And he didn't make it better in a hurry.

"It might be better if you left," he said. "The sheriff's probably right."

Jen had been about to apologize – to thank him – but now the words died in her throat.

For the second time tonight, she felt the sudden onset of tears – with bruises still forming on her face and arms – and all that was left was the humiliation.

She thought she would go absolutely crazy if Daniel saw her cry tonight.

"I'm in," she said curtly – briefly, requiring no breath that might have let out a sob. She fumbled her key into her lock. "See you in the morning," she said.

She disappeared into her room.

And when she peeked out the curtains, she saw Daniel heading to his room without looking back.

CHAPTER 14

Daniel woke the next morning to Wesley calling him, his cell-phone buzzing on his nightstand like a jumping bean.

"Someone broke into the park last night," Wesley said. "That big croc we caught? Someone killed it. Shot it right between the eyes."

"Well," Daniel said. "That didn't take long."

"Quinton's boys?" Wesley asked.

Daniel sighed. "Only three of them went to jail. One of the brothers. I don't know how many hired hands that leaves."

"Enough," Wesley said. "Listen, Daniel, I'm beginning to think you should just get out of there."

Daniel was beginning to think so too.

What *would* be the harm?

If what he really wanted was the croc out of the water, Quinton would certainly get it done. Barnes was not wrong.

So why did Daniel find himself resisting? Just for the sake of Law and Order? Or dutiful determination to 'do his job'? Or perhaps even pride at how good he was at it?

None of that felt right – although pride was probably a closer call. Maybe it was as simple as 'this is my turf' and he wasn't going to be put off of it.

Or maybe... just maybe... he didn't want to let the bad guys win.

Perhaps even *that* was an offshoot of pride – the idea of taking it upon himself – wanting to be a hero.

Was that it? And a hero for who, exactly?

Last night he had acted without thinking. And if he was honest with himself, he should have realized – dense as he could be – there had been potential for a moment he had been pining over for ten years.

He had turned away from that moment – consciously – perhaps even with a touch of hostility – maybe even resentment.

Or, could it be preoccupation with certain tattooed swamp-minx?

"Daniel?" Wesley said. "What do you think?"

Daniel sighed. "Look," he said, "we already have traps out. God willing, that big croc's sitting in one of them right now, and it's over after today."

Another day, he decided. They were already out here.

"Be careful, Daniel," Wesley said.

"Start making your calls, Mr. Wesley," Daniel said, and hung up.

Abigail and Jen were both waiting at the dock.

Jen huddled over a thermos full of motel coffee, glancing up only briefly as Daniel nodded good-morning.

Abigail had settled in her seat at the head of the boat – lounged in that catlike way that managed to turn the rustic and menial into luxury.

As she turned her green eyes on him, Daniel actually felt a little chill.

She was almost stunningly beautiful – in an aggressive, predatory way that Daniel was unaccustomed to.

He would be utterly lying to himself if he didn't admit to some very basic man-thoughts about her. But this was not warm, summer-breeze attraction – more like winter wind and goose-flesh. Witchy woman.

Jen was eyeing him coldly over the steam in her cup.

"Hey! Are we working today?"

Daniel tossed his pack, and clambered aboard after it.

Jen took her middle plank as Daniel started the motor, steering out into the main river. Without being told, he turned in the direction of the lagoon.

Daniel found himself feeling a bit nervous.

That big croc might actually be there.

Daniel had watched footage of that twenty-footer in the Philippines being pulled out of the swamp on a simple wooden cart. At one point, the two-thousand pound beast had death-rolled, scattering villagers, literally tearing the cart to pieces – and would have escaped but for the towels strapped over its eyes.

It had been like watching a damn dinosaur.

He took a deliberately calming breath. Time to be professional.

But when they puttered into the lagoon, the trap was undisturbed.

"Oh, God DAMN it," Abigail said, standing up suddenly.

She threw her rifle to her shoulder and fired.

"What the hell...!" Jen sputtered as the bullet glanced off the cage.

There was a hissing screech and something skittered through the bars of the trap, mouth still full of feathers, and dived into the water.

"Monitor lizard," Abigail said. "Son of a bitch. It got away."

As they grew closer, they could see the live bait they'd left the day before had been devoured right down to the feet.

The Nile monitor was a somewhat underrated invader in the Everglades – a relative of Komodo dragons – a lizard that quite readily took human prey if given the opportunity – and unlike crocodiles, the Komodo patrolled on land – the only reason the death count from dragons was small was because of their isolation and limited range – but where you found them, it happened – there was a highly-publicized account of a young boy snatched from a school yard.

Monitors will tear open the stomach and spread out the contents – eating the best parts first.

This is what the parents would have found.

Likewise, there was a gory incident with Nile monitors – in Delaware of all places. A guy owned several lizards, all purchased off the black-market, and got bit. Turns out, monitors are venomous, and the bite killed him – whereupon the lizards fed upon his corpse for the next several days.

"Boy," Abigail was saying, "I wish I could have gotten that little bastard."

"Do you have to kill everything?" Jen asked.

Abigail glared impatiently.

"That lizard by itself might raid every trap we put out. And there might be more of them." Abigail slapped the boat rail. "Shit!"

She looked back to Daniel. "We need to get some chicken-wire. And more chickens."

"More live bait," Jen muttered.

"The other option," Abigail said, "is bait too big to pull out. Maybe we could find a goat?"

Jen frowned, saying nothing. Daniel took quiet note, that neither did she look to him for support.

"Well," Abigail said, "that kills a whole day." She flopped back down in her seat.

Daniel mentally reevaluated their schedule. He'd half been prepared to leave today – now, he was looking at time spent, back to the cabin, checking the other trap – then back to the main trap in the lagoon, and set up all over again. At least another full day.

As if reading his thoughts, Abigail said, "I could take one of my father's boats out to the other trap."

But Daniel shook his head. He didn't want anyone out on the water alone.

He found himself looking up at the Hanging Tree – the big limb that stretched out over the trap – still with the remnants of a rope swing – frayed, knotted, over twenty years old.

Daniel remembered swings like that as a kid – a tall tree leaning out over some lake – practically designed to hang a rope and a tire.

Until you thought about what waited in the murky water beneath.

CHAPTER 15

They spent the better part of the day resetting both traps. The second had likewise been raided – not even feathers behind this time.

Under Abigail's instruction, they stretched the chicken-wire over the top, attaching it to both sides just under the waterline.

"Those lizards can still get in underwater," she said. "If they figure that out, we'll have to pull the whole cage out, and seal the bottom too."

"Unless," she said, "you feel like going swimming."

Jen remained mostly silent – their terse exchange that morning had been the high-point, and for the rest of the afternoon, she just simply wouldn't engage.

By the time they reached the dock again, Daniel had made a too-long-coming decision – and something inside him broke a little bit.

Part of it was to just stop being silly and acknowledge what had been known and decided within the first thirty-seconds of meeting her – she didn't see him 'that way' – was, is, and always.

So.... finally.... he gave up.

Now the fiction would be to pretend that there had never been anything at all.

Jen didn't speak as she helped him dock the boat and unload the equipment, nor as he professionally and politely helped her with her bag. But as they walked back to the motel together, each turning towards their own rooms, he believed she knew it too.

"Good night, Jen," Daniel said – not angry – even gentle – a touch wistful.

As if to put a stamp on it, Jen turned away, saying nothing.

And whatever torch he had carried was burnt and gone.

Embarrassing that it had taken so long. It really left him feeling rather stupid.

Lost in his own thoughts, he almost bumped into Abigail as she came out of the motel office. He reflexively grabbed her by both shoulders and found himself staring directly into those bizarre emerald eyes.

They seemed to change at her whim – no longer black, the green now dominated – and actually seemed to glow in the neon light of the motel sign.

She tossed her hair in the light breeze – a whisper of wind that pulled at the silk of her shirt like ghostly, groping hands.

She was wearing her pack.

"Where are you going?" Daniel asked.

"Home," she said. "According to the lawyers, it's my place now."

"And maybe a crime scene," Daniel said.

"So call *your* lawyers."

Daniel sighed, conceding the issue completely. He couldn't wait to hand over jurisdiction of this mess to the real cops.

"Besides," Abigail said, "there's rain coming in." She held up her phone, showing a weather bulletin on-screen. "I'm going to get my truck."

"On foot? That's ten miles."

Abigail tipped her head. "Well," she said, "you did promise me a tow."

Daniel shrugged, nodding to his parks vehicle – the boat trailer would double nicely.

"I've got a truck," he said.

He checked his watch. Assuming the flooded roads had receded in the last two days, they could have it well and done in a couple hours.

"Let's go," he said, grabbing her bags and tossing them in the cab. Abigail climbed in beside him.

Daniel wondered if Jen was watching as they pulled out of the parking lot.

The sun had already been fading, but once they got on the road, they quickly lost their daylight – the overhead foliage was like beaded curtains.

They weren't ten minutes along when the rains – slated for later that evening – arrived in full force.

It was that blast of tropical-style rain that hits so hard it's like driving into a waterfall – it was difficult to see the windshield wipers as they swatted the torrential downpour back and forth – their headlights were reflected back in a blinding glare.

"Holy shit," Daniel said, slowing down. "You're lucky you weren't walking in this."

Abigail leaned back, staring out the window. Lightning strikes joined the downpour and her face was lit up in strobe-light flashes.

"This is a big one," Abigail agreed, her face serene, watching the electric light-show as if it were being presented just for her.

Daniel found himself worrying about the roads. If they weren't careful they could wind up on foot anyway. Or swimming.

He had walked through flash-flooding before – once for nearly three miles – the knee-deep current tugging at his legs... and all those little critters sailing by – bugs, vipers, lizards – every now and again, one of them would try to grab onto you as they fought to escape the flood.

Add to that, the torrent of rain and ball-lightning.

For Abigail however, it actually seemed a calming influence – like easy-listening playing on the radio.

They found her truck where she'd left it – the actual distance was two-miles to the cabin.

Daniel stepped out into the deluge and was immediately soaked head to toe – warm, tropical rain, like day-old bathwater, heavy with swamp stench – and then he nearly slipped face-first into the mud as he pulled out the tow-rope.

"Need help?" Abigail asked, cracking her window, looking somehow deliberately warm and comfortable as he toiled on her behalf.

"I'm okay," he said, almost losing his footing again as he attached the cable to Abigail's truck – and was nearly knocked over a third time as a heavy gust yanked his car-door out of his hand, before finally clambering back into the driver's seat.

Utterly drenched and covered in swamp slop, he turned to find Abigail grinning.

"I'm doing you a favor here," Daniel reminded her archly.

Abigail nodded, eyeing him thoughtfully.

"You do a lot of favors, don't you, Ranger? But that's your job, isn't it? It's who you are."

Now the look in her eye became speculative.

"But, I wonder," she said, "whoever does favors for you?"

Daniel said nothing, uncertain where he was being led.

"I told you before," Abigail said, "you've got a little bit of spider in you. Anyone who knows you could see it."

"How so?"

"Like a spider patiently waiting for her prey, the spider-spirit shows your patience – particularly, regarding your long-term goals."

"Okay," Daniel said, "and what would my long-term goal be?"

Abigail looked at him frankly.

"Please," she said. "*Her.* Your little girlfriend back there."

"Jen? No, I'm not..."

But Abigail shushed him with a dismissive wave.

"You've been patiently waiting for her. Probably for years. Just like a spider in your web."

Daniel frowned. He wasn't sure he liked that image – it felt a little predatory.

Is that really what he had been doing? Just sitting there, perched? Waiting for the right moment to pounce?

Sort of like the look in Abigail's eyes right at that very moment?

Those green-eyes were shining black again – the irises expanding in the dark – responding to a rise of pressure – the beat of the heart.

He had never seen anyone's eyes literally glow like that – literally like a cat – reflecting the dash-light, the flash of lightning, like a black-light – eldritch.

It was actually giving him the creeps.

Abigail was smiling at him.

"It's my contacts," she said. "They reflect light. Especially at night." She chuckled. "I've seen that look before."

Daniel quipped brief, relieved laughter. "Okay. Jeez. I thought I was looking at a devil-woman."

Abigail blinked her glowing eyes. "Or maybe you were hoping."

Daniel glanced at his own eyes in the mirror.

They stared back over deep circles – wary and watchful.

"It makes you uncomfortable to talk about it, doesn't it?" Abigail said.

Daniel's silence was answer enough.

"And there's your spirit-animal again," Abigail said. "An act of creation requires integration – and negativity brings discord."

Abigail was sitting up now, looking at him directly.

Daniel deliberately concentrated on the road.

"It highlights things you fear, or dislike about yourself," Abigail said. She reached out and brushed lightly at his hair – the tickle of the spiderweb. "That's why spiders can bring such a sense of unease," she said. "They are a reflection of our own shadow self."

Daniel certainly understood feelings of unease – her touch crackled like a static shock.

"So," Daniel said, clearing his voice, "I'm a spider-sign. Is that like a horoscope thing? You know, like meeting someone in a bar? Like I need to find myself another spider?"

It was an attempt to be flippant – even if it was practically, an admission to everything, as he almost involuntarily tried to steer back into his comfort zone. But Abigail wouldn't allow it.

She was shaking her head sternly.

"The last thing," she said, "that you want is another spider."

"Why's that?"

"Don't you know what happens to the male spider after mating?"

Daniel glanced down at her arms, striped with webs and arachnids.

"So," he said, "just to be clear, that means you and I should never mate?"

Abigail leaned back in her seat, smiling easily.

"Guess not," she said.

Ahead, the foliage began to part. They were coming up to the first major split in the river and the rickety bridge that led over to Abigail's property.

A mile beyond, and they finally reached Ol' Bill's cabin.

Daniel pulled up to the main gate, jumping back out into the storm, letting them through. Then he towed Abigail's truck over to the main garage, unhooking the little pick-up from the cable.

The passage of the river was louder now, flowing less than five feet below the footbridge that led to the main cabin.

Within reach, Daniel thought.

Abigail stepped out of the truck, moving under the barn-roof out of the rain.

Daniel turned to her. "Well," he said, "good night, Abigail."

She smiled back at him indulgently, amused. Then she reached out and took his hand.

"Walk me to my door?" she said. "Come inside?"

"What about the spider-sign?"

Abigail's eyes batted slowly.

"The male spider goes in anyway. Doesn't he?"

She stepped up suddenly close – the movement of the spider scurrying down its web at a trapped fly.

"There's no arguing with nature. Is there?"

Now she rubbed up against to him – the crackle of her touch eliciting the chemical response – pheromones practically popping in the air

"Impairs judgment, doesn't it?" she said.

And Daniel very much understood that mindless male spider – not knowing any better – every instinct telling him to move, yet stayed still and let himself be devoured.

But he was different, wasn't he? He was a man – he had a mind – he *did* know better, right?

He stayed, spider-still as she slipped into his arms.

Apparently not.

She breathed into his ear.

"Let's scratch this itch."

Her lips touched his neck. Her nails traced, teasing, along his skin.

"Come into my parlor," she whispered.

With the electric storm lighting the skies like battling spirits, he took her up in his arms, bracing against the torrent, and carried her into her cabin – feeling the rock of the foot-bridge as it tossed in the wind, barely five feet above the turgid water.

He pushed open the cabin door into the eerie blue light – strobing now, in static pulses with the eldritch flash of the storm.

Abigail was a live weight in his arms – light as a feather – as if she were literally floating on air.

He felt his way to the bedroom in the electric moonbeam, and laid her back on her bed – a girl's room – one she hadn't lived in since she was fifteen.

Daniel was reminded of the last time he was in a room like this – a girl from high-school – his own first time. And this felt just like that – as if he were fifteen again, young, insecure.

He was damn near twice her age, he thought briefly – yet he felt like a teenager with a forty-year old call-girl.

Another one of those compliments he chose not to give her.

Except, he thought, Abigail might have actually liked it.

Her arms came up around him – the entwining whisper of the spider's web.

Her green/black eyes blinked up at him in the spectral dark.

She pulled him down beside her.

And it was... fantastic.

The two of them together – alone out in the primordial swamp – the hoodoo backdrop of the blasting storm – the crash of lightning and the roar of thunder.

It was *primal*.

And sometime later, after it was done, laying in the afterglow, Daniel lay, the contented spider, waiting for what came next.

Abigail lay beside him, serene and softly caressing. Daniel had wondered if she would talk afterwards, but she had fallen silent.

He had thought she had fallen asleep when she suddenly spoke aloud in the dark.

"Quinton was wrong, you know," she said.

Daniel had begun to doze and he started back awake.

"My father," Abigail said, "never fed his boys to a crocodile."

Her hands caressed his chest softly, comfortably.

"*I* did," she said. "And I didn't feed just one. I fed two."

Daniel blinked awake in the dark.

There was a pulse of ice that beat through his heart.

The spider lay under his arm, fuzzy like a dog, but with dripping fangs, and black, unblinking eyes.

Content for now, satisfied in the afterglow, but the moment he moved – the tug at the web...

Daniel lay stone-still as Abigail began to speak.

"Johnny," she said, "Quinton's oldest boy... my mom's ex. HE was the first one."

CHAPTER 16

"I was four years old," Abigail said.

She lay with her head on Daniel's chest as he spoke, clinging to him as if he might try to get away.

"It was dark," she said, "I was sleeping. And something woke me up."

The fingers tracing Daniel's skin moved faster with the memory – he could feel the sharpness of her nails.

"I... had learned not to get up in the middle of the night. The last time... I'd heard arguing... and my mother screamed..."

The tracing nails dug ever so slightly.

"But this time, it was something different. At first it was just voices – not loud – but it sounded like somebody was hurt.

"Or," Abigail said, considering, "maybe someone coming awake." She thought about it – a new take on a memory she'd reviewed a thousand times.

"Either way," she said, "all of a sudden, it got loud. And I heard a loud crack – like someone breaking a brick with a sledge."

Daniel shut his eyes – seeing the image in the dark.

"That escalated," Abigail said, "into steady, thudding blows – like chopping wood."

The tracing fingers dug a little deeper.

"Then, I heard him calling me," Abigail said. "I went out on the front porch and there he was with Johnny.

"Johnny was in a little pile on the dock – all his arms and legs chopped off and piled on top of each other. Blood was running through the cracks in the wood, like when we gutted fish.

"And," Abigail said, "I could see Caesar waiting, just a dozen feet out in the water."

Now Daniel felt just a little tremor as she clung to him,

"That's where he fed him, see? Right off the dock. Sometimes on the bank. You saw the pictures. That big croc would rear right up and snatch food out of his hands."

Keeping his breath deliberately smooth, Daniel's hands rubbed over her soothingly – an almost involuntary action – calming the spider.

"He told it to me like a story," Abigail said. "He pointed to Johnny all piled up on the dock like chattel, and told me, 'That's the guy that took your mother from us.'"

A choke of bitter laughter actually escaped her lips. "He actually seemed to tear-up," she said. "He said Johnny had come to steal my mamma away, and when she wouldn't come, he killed her."

Abigail took a deep breath – the catharsis of confession.

"Then," she said, her voice fading to a whisper, "he made me feed Johnny's pieces to Caesar."

Daniel could no longer shut his eyes – it was worse with his eyes shut. But his fingers betrayed nothing as they massaged and caressed.

"He taught me how," Abigail said. "Getting the croc to focus on the meat. Just like tossing a ball for a dog."

Daniel knew the technique – he had done it himself with gators and frozen chickens. Jen fed salties and Nile crocs every day at Gator Glades.

Thus, he was able to picture very vividly, Abigail, no more than a toddler, waddling to the edge of the dock, a human arm in her hand, and tossing it awkwardly to the waiting beast below. He needed no imagination to picture the massive jaws reaching up – the 'jaw-snap' – and then the limb being tossed, unchewed, down the cavernous gullet.

"After that, Quinton's boys would show up from time to time," Abigail said. "Seems like a lot of other folks, would show up too. For living out so far, seems like there was never a shortage of people that just didn't want to leave us alone. And every now and then, someone would disappear."

Every 'now and then', Daniel thought – a casual phrase – semi-regular.

"Don't get me wrong," Abigail was saying, "Daddy... he wasn't like a serial killer, or anything. It was just those who did him wrong. Or 'cause he HAD to."

Abigail considered.

"That's not to say he might not have jumped the gun, on occasion."

Daniel thought of Jen – how she had caught Ol' Bill feeding the crocs that night – that moment when he'd looked into her eyes as he considered murdering her with the utter callous disregard you might consider putting out a trap for a nuisance animal.

Had Ol' Bill nearly 'jumped the gun', on that occasion?

Jen had no idea how lucky she had really been.

"I guess," Abigail speculated, "once you get started... you know."

She let the point hang with an apathetic shrug.

"It changes you, I guess," she said.

Daniel allowed that was likely true.

"It stopped for a while," Abigail continued. "Once I started getting older, I did most of the in-town errands – it took him off-stage – out of sight, out of mind. It actually seemed like everyone had forgotten about us."

But she shook her head.

"No," she said. "It was just *me* that forgot. Virgil was Johnny's younger brother, and he held it all against us. There was rumor that Daddy had something to do with his brother. That was enough for Virgil."

Go-figure, Daniel thought. 'Rumor'.

"After he came after me," Abigail said, 'Daddy went and got *him*."

Now the tracing nails on Daniel's chest turned into claws. Abigail did not even seem aware as her fingers began to involuntarily clench into Daniel's skin. He suppressed a screech.

"Same as before," Abigail said. "He had him in a pile waiting on the dock. Caesar AND Nemo this time. He looked at me and said, "You know what to do."

A soft chuckle actually escaped her lips.

"Nemo was smaller then. When you were feeding them, you had to make sure he got some – 'cause Caesar would hog it all."

Daniel shut his eyes.

Like treading water, he maintained his slow, calming caress over her back and shoulders – keeping tension off the web.

Abigail lay silent for several minutes, letting Daniel's fingers work, accepting positive stimuli.

"I left home after that," she said, finally. And now, Daniel could feel her body begin to relax. Her hands unclenched, and she settled more comfortably into his arms.

"Seventeen years," she said, and then faded into silence.

Daniel brushed her hair.

After a few more minutes her breath deepened and she slipped away into sleep.

Daniel lay there in the dark, the spider curled under his arm, its sheathed fangs dripping poison, laying there passive and dormant, only until that sudden twitch, when those fangs suddenly come alive and turn upon you.

Abigail slept peacefully beside him.

Daniel lay awake, blinking in the dark.

CHAPTER 17

Daniel must have slept because the next thing he knew, his phone was ringing – Jen's ringtone.

He blinked, looking around, coming aware.

The spider was gone from under his arm. He was alone in the room.

He had lain there for hours – not wanting to disturb the sleeper beside him. He had watched her, breathing softly and contently, through ruby lips that looked so like red, unblinking eyes.

But at some point she left him.

Shaking off his tattered sleep, Daniel fumbled for his phone.

His battery was low, and this far out in the swamp, the reception was foggy.

"Jen?" he said.

"Daniel? Where are you? You... you weren't in your room..."

He heard knowledge in her voice.

"Daniel...," she said, but then her voice choked away.

Daniel was now fully awake, sitting up in bed, looking around for Abigail.

There was blue light coming from the main room – a blinking computer screen – so bizarrely out of place – and to go with it came the creak of a chair, which had paused at the sound of the ringing phone.

The cabin had gone silent, as if hanging on his words.

Daniel had absolutely no idea what he was going to say next until another voice came on the line – an easy, Australian inflection that left a chill in Daniel's blood like dripping snow-melt.

"Hey, there, Ranger," Quinton Marvin's voice said.

"Quinton?" Daniel said. "What's going on?"

"Well," Quinton said, "we want our croc."

"We haven't even got it yet."

"Oh, I know," Quinton said. "Your lady-friend here has pretty much filled us in. I'm just taking out a little insurance in case ya do. See, your friend – Jennifer?" Quinton paused as if for confirmation. "'Jen'? Alright, 'Jen', is going to be coming out with us today. She's going to sort of be our own on-site expert."

"See how things are gonna be?" Quinton said. "You got your team. We got ours. Working together in the spirit of cooperation."

The old poacher's voice was actually apologetic. "See, here, son," he said, "there's millions bein' tossed around here. Ain't that ever gonna get left up to fair competition.

"And besides," Quinton continued, "it's come to my attention that some phone calls have been made in the last few days – phone calls to some higher-ups that upset a lot of people."

Wesley, Daniel thought. Someone's cage had been rattled.

"People that might be your sponsors?" Daniel asked.

"Let's just say, 'the powers-that-be', and leave it at that."

Quinton spit through his teeth. "For what it's worth, son, I think you're a fine man, and I'm sorry it's had to come to this."

Daniel was standing now.

"Quinton, you listen to me. I don't give a shit about that crocodile. If you hurt her..."

Daniel faded off – actually choked off.

Jen's brief hesitant stammer played over and again in his head.

The night before, he'd given up on her – accepted it. Now the thought of someone hurting her clenched his throat up in near-helpless, choking rage – he found himself unable to even speak – even to threaten.

And Quinton continued to speak in that maddeningly-likable, cut-your-losses, consoling tone.

"Don't get me wrong, boy," he said, "this is strictly a business transaction."

"Suppose I call the sheriff."

"Well, son," Quinton said, "I think you might find the arm of the law ain't as long as you might think. Not out here. You're the law, yourself, after all."

The old trapper chuckled. "I've lived illegally a good portion of my life. And one thing I've learned is that you can only do that if you're allowed to."

Daniel sighed. There was no doubt Barnes had been discouraging, to say the least.

"I'm sure Councilman Wesley won't be happy, either."

"Possibly not," Quinton said. "I guess you have to decide what you want to tell him, don't you?"

Daniel said nothing.

"We're on the water now," Quinton told him. "Trust me when I say we don't want to play this game with each other. Nope – we just want to work together."

"If you touch her..." Daniel began again, but Quinton shushed him.

"As far as your girl goes," he said, "our intentions are purely professional."

Quinton considered.

"Although," he continued, "she is a pretty one. And of course, it's early, and the boys ain't really started drinking yet."

Quinton chuckled amiably. "Tell ya, what – you best be puttin' a shake in it."

The phone beeped as Quinton hung up.

Daniel was getting dressed when he looked up to see Abigail standing at the door.

She was already dressed. Behind her, the computer screen had been shut off, leaving her outlined in shadow – a spectral figure – her rifle slung over one shoulder like a scythe.

Daniel looked up at her helplessly.

"They've got Jen," he said.

Abigail nodded.

Daniel tried to gauge the look in her eye – angry? Jealous?

"Well," she said, "if they took her, then you're going to have to take her back. Aren't you?"

"They want the croc."

Abigail shrugged.

"So let's give it to them. Should be easy enough. The traps have been out overnight. Ol' Caesar ought to be waiting in one of them today." She shrugged. "Let's go."

The night's rains had flooded the area. Daniel glanced at his truck, parked opposite the foot-bridge and realized that the road he'd taken in was likely impassable.

They were on their own out here.

Down by the dock, Abigail had already pulled one of her father's boats out of the boathouse, and was waiting next to the dock. But now she brought out a smaller rowboat, and pushed it into the water.

"I'll take the rowboat, here," she said, "and check the trap down river. You go check the lagoon." She held up her phone. "Whoever finds something, call."

Daniel looked unhappily at the diminutive craft she'd purloined for herself. He thought about mentioning the kayaker in Africa. He knew Jen would have.

Abigail was watching him expectantly, her blinking eyes currently emerald green – relaxed morning eyes – but as feral as any staring out of the morning 'glades.

Daniel had not often encountered intelligence in combination with true amorality. It was a factor that simply could not be gauged – to be perfectly aware of strictures, societal mores – yet, utterly unaffected by them.

Right now, his life might depend on this woman – not to mention Jen's.

The spider-sign, Abigail had told him, would highlight feelings of discord – even dread.

Daniel was breaking his own rule – he was putting himself in striking distance.

Abigail had opened the main gate, pulling both boats down to the river. She settled into her little rowboat like a kid on a skateboard.

Daniel fired up the battle-scarred outboard – Ol' Bill's cruising wagon – full of ropes and harpoon darts – just like the ones Quinton had used – as well as a decorative layer of swamp scum and the smell of carrion and fish guts.

Abigail was eyeing him seriously.

"You might just be finding something out there today," she said. She pointed to the pistol on his hip. "Don't be shy."

"They want it alive," Daniel said.

Abigail frowned, saying nothing.

Daniel started to push into the current. Abigail turned her paddles, steering the little rowboat in the opposite direction.

But before she began to row, she turned back over her shoulder.

"They want the croc, alright," she said. "But don't kid yourself that'll be enough."

She hefted her own rifle, nodding meaningfully at Daniel.

"Don't be shy," she said.

"Be careful, Abigail," Daniel said.

Then he revved the motor, steering into the main current.

Abigail watched him go, waiting until he had turned the bend out of sight before she began to row.

About a hundred yards down-river, she pulled the little boat over to the bank. Picking a leafy patch, she settled in, discreetly out of sight – just like a spider in a web – with a full view of both her cabin and the approaching river.

She sat – just like a spider.

Watching.

Waiting.

CHAPTER 18

Jen had to hand it to Quinton Marvin – his lackadaisical air was deceptive – his amiable ramble and distracted yarning belied a shrewd, observant eye.

In that way, he was a bit like a croc, himself. He lulled you, caught you with your guard down. When he'd kidnapped her early that morning, he'd done so without laying a finger on her. He had simply knocked on her door. Bleary with disgruntled sleep, she had answered without the slightest thought. He and Nigel had stepped inside. A third beefy shadow – likely Mathew – hovered outside.

"Let's not make this any harder than it has to be."

They had ushered her to the dock, where three boats waited – Pete and Mathew loaded into the big one, a smaller outboard for Nigel. And the third sat empty and waiting.

"Start checking all our traps," Quinton said to the others. "And all of theirs. Anybody finds anything, call."

He pointed specifically to Pete and Mathew. "You two," he said, "know what to do."

He turned to Jen. "You're with me girl."

He handed her a spotlight, and nodded to the bow.

"If you wouldn't mind navigating."

Jen said nothing, taking the spotlight and assuming her seat at the head of the boat.

They were already out on the water when Quinton made his call to Daniel – Daniel, whose truck she had noticed missing from the parking lot outside the motel.

And yes, she *had* seen him driving off with Abigail last night.

There was no one there, even if she had tried to call for help.

So instead, she found herself spirited off by this swamp-pirate, out into the Everglades alone.

It was still dark when they reached the Hanging Tree.

"Early bird," Quinton said.

As they trolled into the clearing, Jen turned the beam up and over the water, hunting for the tree, and Abigail's trap.

"See," Quinton explained, "it'll all just be better if we get that big croc first – rather than having to dicker and all. Ol' Abigail might try to lay claim – her trap after all."

Jen was shaking her head. "At this point, how could you possibly care about legalities?"

"Ain't 'legalities' so much," Quinton said, "as what Ol' Abby might do if she feels she's got rights."

Quinton frowned. "Yeah," he said, "things really got fouled up when Ol' Bill's girl decided to show up again. Didn't really expect that."

He turned a solemn eye to Jen.

"But as far as the law goes? Well, you could say I'm acting on the law – the REAL law. Because I'm all there is out here, and there's some powerful people that want this business good and done.

"See," he said, "I'm just making sure things get done right. Trust me girl, I'm trying to look out for everybody."

"Is that why you kidnapped me?"

"Why do you think I decided to keep you here with me instead of the boys?"

As he spoke, he noted the bruises Nigel had left, still mottled on her arms.

The old poacher's eyes softened with regret.

"What can I say?" Quinton shrugged. "I wish I could tell you I didn't raise him that way. But I guess I did."

Jen turned away, folding her arms – the helpless shame left by the marks flushing her face.

Quinton appeared about to speak, but held his tongue.

As they steered into the cove, the spotlight beam had found the Hanging Tree – the rope swing dangled, sopped in last night's torrent.

And the waters were flooded, uprooting the trap below – it looked like the floating cage had hooked itself along the main trunk of the tree.

But even in the dark, even in the distance, they could both see the gate had been sprung.

Inside the trap, floating just at the water-line, was a knobbed, craggy back.

Quinton's voice was flat and deadly calm – the old-time croc-trapper.

"There he is," he said.

CHAPTER 19

It was big. REAL big.

Jen had seen the attack video on the fisherman, so she knew they were dealing with a large animal, but in person...

The big croc – Caesar – was mostly submerged, with just its back plates and eyes showing. But its back was so WIDE – it was like a sandbank.

Jen could only guess its weight – over a ton?

It sat, apparently placid, inside the cage – although as they drew closer, there appeared to be a ripple in the metal bars – as if with some effort to thrash its way loose as it had before.

But this trap had been built for him – built by his daddy.

Still, Jen found herself doubtful.

The size difference was notable – she had seen eighteen-foot crocs, and this one was easily that – yet this animal had BULK.

On a normal day, she would have simply secured the cage, and called a whole team from the park or the ranger's station – they would have been on the news.

As opposed to trying to wrangle this thing with a couple of whiskey-soaked hillbillies.

Quinton seemed impressed.

"He's a monster, ain't he?" He steered them in closer, pulling lengthwise along the cage, which stretched out several feet past the bow.

"Looks like he made a fair-attempt to get away, too."

Jen said nothing, but to her eye, it actually looked like the mooring of the cage had been torn loose – evidently from just thrashing around from within – and the trap itself had been caught on a low hanging branch – just under the waterline after last night's flooding – or else it would have simply floated off with the current.

Quinton rapped his knuckles on the pontoons running along the edge of the trap.

"Boy, she made it easy for us, didn't she?" He laughed. "Practically, all we've got to do is tow it in."

Quinton pulled experimentally where the branch had hooked the trap.

"Provided we can get it loose, that is." He smiled at Jen. "Looks like we're gonna need some help."

He pulled out his phone, holding it up as a speaker. Nigel's voice answered.

"Got somethin', Daddy?"

"Oh yeah," Quinton said. "Over by the Tree. Biggest bastard I've ever seen. But I'm gonna need a little muscle to get him loose."

"Be there in a minute," Nigel said.

Quinton pocketed his phone, smiling amiably to Jen. "He'll be along."

Jen looked at the animal waiting in the trap.

In typical croc fashion it sat utterly still – not an iota of energy being spent.

But its eyes watched them. Jen had seen those eyes every day at Gator Glades and she knew they missed absolutely nothing – they didn't get distracted or bored – they just watched.

Until you were close enough.

Then they moved with speed that was as shocking as it was sudden.

A croc's jaws snapped shut in a third of a second. They could leap their full body length forward out onto the beach from sitting dead still.

Jen tried to imagine the power of the beast that sat so deceptively calm before her – what it could do if given even a second.

She ran her hand along the cold metal bars where they had been distended and distorted – to her hand, they might as well have been welded.

Daniel had sent her a video once, of a big croc that had seized the nose of a mid-sized elephant calf. Nile crocs often made the mistake of grabbing the trunks of elephants drinking at the river, belatedly discovering a much larger animal at the other end – in point of fact, these unfortunate crocs often didn't survive the encounter, sometimes being discovered in the top branches of trees.

But *this* Niley was big, and the elephant was small – it had stumbled and nearly fallen into the river face-first.

Luckily, the young pachyderm had recovered and pulled both itself and the croc out of the water. But that was a fourteen-foot croc that had nearly taken an elephant.

THIS thing...

Jen was afraid.

It was almost ridiculous to say – here she was, kidnapped, out on the 'glades, in the darkest hours of the morning – NOT being afraid would be idiotic.

But this was different – this was... primordial.

Never once had she felt like this over an animal – for fifteen years, she walked by five-meter salties every day – it was like machinery – just keep your hands clear.

But here, she shrank back – the instinctive reaction of a prey animal.

Quinton evidently read it in her eyes.

"He's got you bedeviled, doesn't he?"

Jen glared back at him, granting nothing.

"No shame in it, honey," Quinton said. "Creature like this? You better be afraid."

But then he shook his head reassuringly. "Don't worry. There really ought not be anything to it. He's already caught. We just got to get him loose of that tree to get him towed." He shrugged. "Then we're all done."

Jen stared back at him, and almost asked the next question – what then?

Quinton was a sensible enough fellow – within his perimeter, anyway – and Jen could see no sensible reason to let her live.

In fact, if she had to put a bet to it, she and Daniel were both likely scheduled to disappear in the swamp at the conclusion of this little hunt. Probably that skank little swamp slut too.

Sure, Wesley might kick up a fuss, but Quinton could make up any story he liked.

And if there really were 'powerful players' involved – whatever that meant – money, for sure – likely politics – maybe even law-enforcement – Sheriff Barnes, anyone? – Jen could see any number of excuses for no one ever finding out what had happened here.

In a way, it was almost funny that she found herself more afraid of the crocodile.

Go-figure. She still jumped at spiders, too. That really didn't make much sense either.

In the belch and burble of the swamp, came the sound of a second boat motor.

After a moment, the light from Nigel's outboard came into view.

"Damn!" Nigel exclaimed as he pulled up next to the trap. "He IS one big bastard, isn't he?"

"And he's ours, if we hurry," Quinton said. "We gotta get him loose off that tree."

Nigel glanced around. "Where's Pete?"

"Pete's on his own errands," Quinton said, glancing at Jen quickly. "Don't worry about Pete. Just get a damn line over that branch."

96

Nigel tossed a length of rope over the long limb of the Hanging Tree, and then looped it around the cage bars, where it had hooked just at the base of the trunk. He gave it an experimental tug.

"That's wedged on there good, Daddy," Nigel said.

"Here," Quinton said, "let's get a little muscle into it." He smiled at Jen. "Come on, girl. You're a strong one, ain't ya?"

With both boats on either side of the trap, and Nigel pulling for all he was worth on the rope, Quinton and Jen leaned into the bars.

Jen calculated the weight of the cage – a thousand pounds? It was caught at an angle – the tree was just bracing it – she could even see the nub of a branch, about four-feet under the surface, that had hooked the corner like a shoe-horn.

"We need to come up about a foot," Jen said. "But I can't get any leverage."

Pulling the boat closer to the tree, Quinton reached one leg over the side, finding where the main trunk angled its way underwater – he found a notch to place his feet, while grabbing hold of the cage like a weight-lifter doing a dead-lift.

"Everybody!" he grunted. "Pull!"

Nigel strained on the rope, and Jen struggled as best she could with the poor footing.

The cage remained as immovable as a rock.

Quinton's face was turning purple – for an old codger, he was as corded as wire rope.

"Come on!" he growled, straining.

The cage shifted – not loose but it suddenly jerked up half-a-foot.

Jen looked below the surface where the cage was now mounted on the top of the branch stub rather than hooked on it.

"Almost," she said.

Quinton took a breath. "Okay," he said grabbing the bars again, "once more."

At that moment, Caesar, who had been watching the proceedings apathetically, suddenly rolled.

With a two-thousand pound animal inside, the cage rolled with it.

"Ohhh shit!" Quinton yelled as the metal bar he'd just gripped so tightly suddenly jerked and pitched him bodily out into the water. He actually crested in the air before landing with a loud splash a dozen yards into the marsh.

Nigel was likewise yanked into the air by his own rope, letting go just barely before being dragged face-first into the overhanging branch. He toppled over backwards into the water. He came up, floundering.

Jen had taken a stiff bar to the face, before being pancaked back into the water.

She landed on her back, her scalp bleeding, nearly knocked-out, and she began to sink.

Probably, she would have drowned had the cage not continued to roll, catching the railing of the boat she'd just been thrown out of, flipping the whole thing upwards in the water.

The boat came down right between Jen's shin and ankle – and it was only the screaming pain of breaking bone that jerked her awake enough to thrash in the water.

She sputtered and choked before finding the surface, gasping for air.

When she started to kick water, a bolt of pain shot through her fractured leg.

Beside her, the cage had slid free from its perch under the tree. One of the pontoons was loose and the trap was listing badly, its top now almost completely underwater.

Jen actually felt a moment of concern – if the cage sank to the bottom with the croc inside it, it would drown.

Then she realized that wouldn't be a problem.

The cage floated freely... and empty.

Its trap door was sprung wide open.

"Oh my God," Jen whispered.

Ignoring the agony in her ankle, Jen begin to swim for the tree.

Nigel was standing on his own overturned boat.

"I don't see him!" he was shouting.

Quinton shouted back as he swam. "Get up the tree, ya' damned fool!"

Glancing around at the murky brine, Nigel hopped deftly from the overturned boat, and grabbed on to the wide trunk.

Jen felt Quinton's hands on her as she struggled in the water.

"Easy, girl," he said. "I gotcha. Ya took a blow, it looks like."

Jen blinked, still not fully aware. She touched her forehead and it came up bloody.

"I think my foot's broken," she said.

Quinton waved at Nigel. "Here, boy, help the lady."

They were pushing past the overturned boats and Nigel caught Jen's outstretched hand. She cried out as the movement jostled her leg.

Quinton eyed the water warily as Nigel helped Jen up onto the overhanging branch.

"What ya think?" he said. "Maybe he made a run for it. Maybe gettin' caught spooked him."

Nigel reached down for his father's hand, his own eyes scanning the flat surface.

"Yeah," he said. "I'm sure that's it. We're probably perfectly fine. Just get up on the branch, ya old bastard."

Jen bent her injured foot up on the branch beside her. The ankle was already dark purple and swollen.

Quinton shuffled up on the branch next to her, and poked at it gingerly.

"Keep away from me," Jen shouted, skirting back.

Quinton held up placating hands. "Just checkin' you over, girl. Trust me, I'm not your biggest problem."

He glanced down where Nigel was reaching for the boat rope. Both boats had been capsized, and Quinton's had taken a deep hole where the cage had struck, - it had actually started to up-end as it sank. Nigel's boat, however, was just overturned.

"If I can get it flipped..." he said, reaching.

"Damn it, Nigel, forget the damned boat and get up here."

Nigel glanced around at the water. "I still don't see him. Maybe he *did* take off."

Nevertheless, he hopped back into the crook of the tree.

"No need," Quinton said, glancing reassuringly at Jen, "No need to get risky. Someone'll be along soon enough. Anybody got a working cell-phone?"

Jen glared. *"You've* got mine."

"Oh, right," Quinton reached for his pocket and pulled out a smashed I-phone. "Well," he said, "that was mine." He patted his pockets. "I guess yours must be somewhere out there in the drink." He glanced down at Nigel, who was starting to climb up beside them.

"You got your phone, Nigel?"

Nigel paused, reaching for his pocket. He held it up. "Water-proofed," he said. He tapped the screen awake. "Hold on," he said.

He had started poking keys when Caesar suddenly reared up right beside the boat, grabbing him by the leg.

Nigel had time for one startled, "Oh shit," before he was yanked below the surface.

He made a small splash.

Quinton made as if to move after him then stopped.

"Boy..." he started – reflexively angry – admonishing.

Then he shut his eyes.

Jen heard a deep breath, that in another man, might have been a sob.

With Quinton it was a muttered curse.

"Damn, boy," he said.

Another deep breath. And then a whisper.

"Damn, damn, damn."

Perched on the branch, Jen and Quinton both scanned the muddy water.

But the still surface revealed nothing.

"Damn," Quinton whispered again.

CHAPTER 20

It was a long time before Quinton spoke again.

Dawn had sent its first splinters out over the water, and the old trapper had lit up one of his awful cigarettes – had 'em all handy with matches in a water-proofed bag – and now he leaned back against the trunk, his feet up as if reclining on his back porch.

Jen had watched him swallow the death of his son right in front of him like a shot of castor oil – a cool, collected veteran.

Now he nodded in her direction. "How's the foot?"

"Hurts like a son of a bitch," Jen replied curtly.

"I only ask, because I'm trying to calculate our options. It might make a difference how hobbled you are. Could you walk on it?"

Jen glanced at the purple swelling club that had replaced her lower leg.

"Given no other option, I would," she said.

"That's a 'no'." Quinton puffed sulfur. "See, I've been thinking of running down there and flipping that boat back over."

Quinton nodded out over the water. "Now, we're a bit tardy on that. Best time would have been right after..." Quinton cleared his throat, and in the manner of a man squaring his shoulders, said it flat-out. "Right after he grabbed Nigel, we might have had a window where we could have moved.... while he still had his mouth full."

The old trapper's eyes darkened a little, with his own deliberately brutal words.

Jen remembered what he'd told her before: "It's always someone you know."

She actually felt a bit bad for the old bastard.

"Thing is," Quinton continued, "we've maybe tarried a little too long, now. He might've been gone, taken a nap, been back again." He shook his head in self-reproach. "I didn't jump on it right away, because I was thinking the other fellas would be along, sooner or later."

Quinton puffed more black tar.

"That and... well... I guess I just needed a minute."

Another deep puff.

"But now that I'm thinking on it, Pete and Mathew might be hours before they even think of looking for us, let alone pick the right spot." Quinton shook his head. "I just wish we hadn't broken the damned cell-phone." He shook his head. "Funny how you start depending on these little trinkets. Fifty years ago we wouldn't have gotten into this fix."

"Daniel will come," Jen reminded him – and actually felt a little bit energized saying so – especially after watching him handle Nigel the other night.

Nigel looked pained. "Yeah... about that." He cleared his voice unhappily. "Ol' Ranger might have a problem getting here from the direction he's comin'."

"See," he explained, "after last night's blow – once the water gets this high – that route to the lagoon from Ol' Bill's spot gets blocked off by the trees. And once they get down by the waterline? I tell ya, it's a bad spot to get caught if the current's strong. There's been more than one poor bastard that didn't make it out.

"And," Quinton said, with a deep drag of black smoke, "I might've had ol' Pete and Mathew knock down a tree or two 'cross the water that direction. Just to make sure."

"Of course you did," Jen said.

Quinton exhaled the smoke slowly, letting it drift, while he mentally did the math.

"So," he said, "comin' from Abigail's he's gonna have to go way back upriver. And that's *after* he figures out he can't make it." He tossed off a finger count. "That's gonna be a couple-few hours, either way."

Jen said nothing, but her lips pursed at 'comin' from Abigail's.

Quinton's quick trapper's eyes caught it.

"You don't like that he spent the night with Abigail, do ya?"

Quinton shook his head, tapping his ash into the water.

"Well, honey," he said, "I dare-say, you're right not to like it." He looked at her sincerely. "My personal opinion is that he'd be a damn fool to let you go."

But then he paused on the thought, considering.

"Or," he said, "maybe he didn't. Maybe it was more the other way around."

Jen stared back at him balefully.

Quinton took another drag of black tar, and now he sat up from the crook of the tree, cracking his back, in the manner of a man getting back to work.

"In any case," he said, "I don't particularly want to be in this... 'position' when your boyfriend shows up."

"He's not my boy..."

But Quinton shushed her, tossing his hand dismissively.

"The point," he said, "is that right now I'm wondering if I want to wait and see who shows up first – mine or yours."

"What else have you got in mind?"

"Well," he said, "we might still have a window to get that boat up-ended."

"You're welcome to try," Jen said. "I'll wait here."

"Well," Quinton said, "if I manage to get that boat over, you're coming with me. And we ain't going to argue about it."

Jen glared back. She would argue.

"But that brings me to my last point," Quinton continued. "See, another reason I wasn't ready to jump in right away was because I wasn't sure if that big croc wasn't being territorial – he might've looked at getting' caught in that trap as pickin' a fight."

He nodded out over the water. Flat. Murky, no reflection. No wind.

"If he was just grabbin' Nigel for something to eat, we'd probably still be okay. He ain't gonna need more than that right away – no need to spend the energy."

"But...." Quinton looked doubtful, "... if he's bein' territorial – well, he could be sitting right below, waiting for us."

Jen looked down at the brown water beneath them.

She found herself thinking of the fisherman on the boat. Grabbed from ten feet.

How high were they now?

Fifteen? Sixteen feet?

"I suppose," Quinton said, thoughtfully, "if I were the sort of person you think I am, I could just toss you in and see."

Jen stared back, eyes wide.

But Quinton smiled – a touch bitterly.

"Don't worry, girl," he said, "I couldn't be THAT big a sonofabitch, could I?"

"I was nearly killed because of you," Jen said. "My life is in danger. All so you could make some money."

Quinton took a final deep drag, burning the brimstone to its noxious-root, and pitched the butt over the side.

"Well, girl," he said, "if it makes you feel any better, it was never really about the money. And if it ever was, it sure isn't now. I'm in it to kill that croc."

"Once a poacher, always a poacher," Jen responded.

"We all find our value in the world, don't we?"

"If that's value."

Quinton smiled. "You know, despite your best efforts, I can't help but like you, girl. You're bright. Ya got a kind heart. Maybe a bit naive – and for some bizarre reason, I don't want you thinkin' badly of me."

Jen was dumbfounded. "Are you kidding?" She waved her arms at the swamp around them. "This!" she said, her voice raising. "THIS is violence. This is a crime."

"No doubt," Quinton replied. "It's also the lesser of two evils."

"What does that mean?"

Quinton's smile faded sadly. "Trust me, girl," he said. "There's a lot of evils out there. And it's just like the crocs. It's the ones you don't see comin'."

The old trapper sighed. "But right now, we just got to keep from dyin', don't we?" He nodded towards her, brows raised. "I don't suppose you've got any ideas?"

Jen actually found that she didn't.

"Well," Quinton said, "I'm gonna get that boat." And then he began to move towards her on the branch.

Jen shrank back, already knowing there was going to be no way to fight him. Maybe she could kick him off the branch.

But instead he reached under the branch for the tattered old rope swing.

"I don't suppose Abigail ever told you why this was called the 'Hanging Tree'?"

He held up the rope.

"The story was, Ol' Bill would dangle people he didn't like out over the water – feedin' 'em to his crocs."

Quinton smiled. "One of those 'rumors'," he said.

And then he swung down on the rope, under the branch and landed on the overturned boat hull.

"Should be right quick," he said, looking up at her. "Get 'er flipped back over and get the hell out of here."

He glanced down at the water.

"The trick," he said, "is to do it without getting eaten."

With that, he hopped over the side, slipping into the water with barely a ripple. Deftly, he found the boat's edge, caught some footing along the base of the tree, and flipped the boat over in the manner of a trained cowboy flipping a steer.

Quinton climbed back into the boat and yanked the motor to life. He looked up at Jen.

"Alright," he said, "let's go, girl. Let's get the hell out of here."

Jen hesitated – to go with him was to stay a captive.

She knew, however, that he would force the issue.

He also wasn't being patient.

"Come on, hon," he said, "don't make me come get ya."

Jen had actually started to move – better on the boat than stuck in this goddamn tree – but the outboard was suddenly hit hard from below.

Quinton was flipped up into the air once again, and this time the boat frame shattered. As Quinton landed with a splash, the motor choked and quit.

"Ah, bloody hell," Quinton sputtered, and started swimming for the tree.

He didn't get ten feet before something jerked him from below.

Just briefly, Jen caught his eye – surprised at first, and then pretty damn pissed off.

He turned to fight something in the water.

Jen heard him speak once more – defiant: "Oh, you miserable bastard!"

Then he was yanked below the surface.

CHAPTER 21

Abigail hadn't long to wait

She actually hadn't expected to – and sure enough, once she'd hunkered her little boat down behind the brush, it was not half-an-hour after Daniel disappeared downriver before a boat came motoring up.

On board, Quinton's son, Pete, and burly Mathew.

Apparently, their errands today were not restricted to checking traps.

Abigail watched as they pulled up to her front dock and let themselves onto the property.

She slipped her boat silently into the river – the dip of her oars just another part of the drip-drip that came from being in the swamp.

Concealed by darkness, Abigail slipped up to the dock behind them, as Pete and Mathew made their way up to the cabin.

Pete was carrying two canisters of gasoline.

Mathew had his rifle out as he nudged open the back door.

Abigail could see the blue electric light emanating from the cabin, broken by shadow, as Mathew did a quick search. She heard his voice a moment later.

"Nobody here," he said. "Let's get it done."

Mathew turned back to the door and Abigail met him in the forehead with the butt of her rifle. The big, hairy hominid dropped like a stone.

Wide-eyed, Pete gaped back at Abigail.

"Abby...?" he began, but she cut him off with another heavy blow to Mathew's head – this one making a cracking sound.

Mathew kicked like a clubbed fish.

Abigail turned the rifle, business-end up, onto Pete.

"Gonna burn me out?" she said. "Worried Ol' Bill might have left a few footprints?"

Pete was shaking his head. "I don't know anything. I swear, Abby – I'm just doing what I was told."

He looked at her pleadingly.

"Abby... I'm sorry... about all that with Virgil. I always *liked* you."

Abigail was unmoved.

"Of course you did," she said. "You wanted to fuck me. Just like your brother. You just never quite had the guts to *take* it."

Abigail's eyes narrowed.

"See, I don't think you're really that different from your brother at all."

"Abby," Pete said, shaking his head, "it ain't like that..."

But she cut him off with her raised rifle.

"Let's get something straight," she said. "Don't pretend we're friends. Don't pretend that I even like you – or that I give a shit if you 'feel bad' for what your brother did. I don't think you're cute, or funny, or even pathetic. All you are to me is meat off a gene-pool I would gut from the planet."

Pete blinked.

"You're going to answer some long-standing questions for me," Abigail said.

"Abby," Pete began, stammering, "I swear – I don't know anything..."

She shut him up with a rifle butt across the face, knocking him to the floor. He rolled over moaning, as Abigail leaned over and grabbed him by the hair, putting the rifle barrel in his face.

"This is how it's going to go," she said. "I'm going to ask you questions and you're going to answer them. If I think you're holding out on me, I'll cut you, and hurt you, and make you scream, and I don't even care IF you talk to me."

Pulling him by the hair, Abigail sat him up into her father's easy chair.

She lowered the rifle barrel to his leg.

"First time you lie to me," she said, "the kneecap goes."

She leaned forward. "Understand?"

Pete nodded, wide-eyed.

Abigail proceeded to ask her questions. And Pete talked.

He told her everything he knew.

She made sure of it.

Out there where no one could hear.

CHAPTER 22

Jen huddled motionless, not daring to move.

In the time since Quinton Marvin had been taken, Caesar had made two attempts at her.

She had clung to the branch for an indeterminate time after the old poacher was pulled under – maybe an hour – simply frozen, unable to move.

However long it had been, she came back into herself by degrees – and finally, she had sat up, looking down at the rippleless surface.

She was scratched and cramped from clinging to the slippery branch – shifting her legs, she shuffled closer to the main trunk.

As she swung her awkward club-foot, pain squirting tears from her eyes, Caesar had risen straight up, breaking the water with barely a ripple, and suddenly the tooth-studded maw was right in her face.

Croc 'jaw-snaps' can be heard over a greater distance than a shotgun blast, and Jen felt the displaced air and splash of water as the teeth snapped shut less than a foot away.

She scrambled on the moss-covered branch and nearly fell in.

Screaming aloud, her ankle an auger of pain, Jen skittered up next to the trunk as Caesar crashed back down into the brine.

The big croc dropped out of sight, briefly, but then reappeared at the surface, its eyes already gauging the distance of its missed strike.

It could reach the branch, Jen realized.

Which meant if she stayed sitting, nearly her whole body was in striking range.

Struggling on the slippery bark, Jen worked her way into a standing position, balanced on her one good foot.

Now only her FEET were in range.

She had begun to do the math in her own head. Quinton estimated potentially hours before *his* boys showed. What about Daniel?

How long had it been since Quinton had made his little ransom call? Even assuming Daniel anticipated the flooding and took the longer-route right from the beginning – *and*, she thought archly, the starting point being Abigail's cabin – how long before he showed up here?

It would, likely, be his first stop. She was pretty sure.

Unless that little swamp-bitch talked him out of it.

Jen shifted weight on her leg – balance was chancy on the slippery branch and was rapidly becoming exhausting. There was also no real grip on the main trunk to take any of her weight.

For a moment, her balance wavered and she slipped.

At that split second, the water below erupted again – not smooth this time, but an all-out attack – the jaws smashed into the bark at the spot she had just removed her foot.

There was a titanic tug, as Caesar latched onto the tree branch itself, and tried to roll.

The big old tree actually strained as it resisted.

Jen thought she heard the slightest creak where the big branch hooked onto the tree – just at her feet.

She shut her eyes, doing more math – two-thousand pounds of torquing muscle, versus an aging branch.

Six inches from her good foot, Caesar's jaws unlatched and the big croc again dropped back into the water.

Jen tucked herself into the crook of the tree, not daring to move.

How long, she wondered, could *this* go on?

It would just wait. It would gather energy and try again, and then try again, and eventually she'd get tired and she would become sufficiently inattentive for it to grab her. If no one came, it could wait for days – hell, if it wanted to, it could wait weeks.

Jen was guessing the best she could do before she collapsed from exhaustion was hours.

She would just have to hope Daniel would be along – and she was just thinking she would perhaps be willing to forgive a tryst with some slutty swamp-bitch if he showed up any time soon, when she lost her balance and simply flipped off the branch into the water.

There was a moment of free-fall, just as she started to tumble and realized she was going over – it was a moment of utter awareness – utter terror – like falling into an open canyon.

She hit the water with an awkward splash.

Almost right beside her, Caesar actually seemed taken aback – apparently prepared to settle down for a long wait with a slippery prey, when it plopped right down almost into his mouth.

She had landed right at the big croc's shoulder, and the jaws came reaching back, even as the big tail came forward – crocs would literally club prey right into their mouths – and that would have been the end of it, except that Jen had also fallen between Caesar, and the half-sunken cage.

The jaws couldn't quite reach her and the tail smashed into the cage.

Grabbing hold of the bars as the entire trap rolled in the water, Jen pulled herself over the top.

There was a loud CLANG as the jaws impacted metal, coming after her, and another shotgun-blast jaw-snap bare inches from her face.

Tumbling over the other side into the water, she found herself face to face with the open hatch.

Jen slipped into the cage like a fish into a hole – pulling the hatch down behind her.

The massive tail crashed down again, ringing in her ears like a tower bell. Then there was another snap of jaws, latching onto the bars, giving the demolished trap a mighty shake.

Tossed inside like dice, Jen felt warm blood running down her face.

For the moment, the pontoons held, but her little space in the cage only allowed her about two feet above the water.

Just on the other side of the bars, Caesar sidled up beside her, his eager yellow eye blinking with intent.

And patience. He had been caught by surprise once, and his prey had eluded him. Now he had learned.

Soon he would begin banging on the cage again, either sinking it, or driving her out.

Jen shut her eyes.

That was when she heard the buzz of a boat motor.

She opened her eyes and saw Daniel, steering into the lagoon.

Not the park's boat, she noted – it was from Abigail's garage.

Jen could see him pause, standing, shielding his eyes from the crest of morning sun rising behind the Hanging Tree.

Beside her, Caesar bumped her cage, as he suddenly turned in the water.

The big croc slipped under the surface, angling towards Daniel and what Jen now realized was a pathetically over-matched boat.

"Jen?" Daniel called, struggling to see in the glare. "Are you there?"

Jen threw her head up in the air and screamed.

"Daniel! Watch out! It's coming for you!"

Daniel's head jerked in her direction, and he dropped to his seat, cranking the motor, looking around warily at the water around him.

Thus, he saw it coming when Caesar exploded out of the water after him.

CHAPTER 23

Without Jen's warning, it would have got him.

The jaws were fully three feet long, and they curled over the bow of his boat at the same moment the tail swiped inward from the back.

But Jen's shout had been enough – once he saw the teeth, he knew the tail would be coming and he threw himself to the bottom. The jaws snapped shut just above his head and the tail struck the boat itself a heavy blow, nearly knocking the motor loose.

This was Ol' Bill's craft – reinforced for just such occasions, but this was a powerful animal – two more strikes like THAT, and it might as well have been balsa wood. Daniel grabbed the motor, and cranked it blindly, launching the boat into a wide, circling arc.

Pulling himself back into his seat, he looked back to see Caesar had disappeared below the surface.

Daniel's hand dropped to the butt of his revolver. Abigail had told him not to be shy, and he had no intention to.

Caesar, unfortunately, was not shy either, rising up underneath, nearly throwing Daniel overboard – and succeeding at knocking the gun out of his hand, where it bounced once on the rail, once on the motor, and then plopped right into the water.

Daniel stared after it mutely.

Really wish THAT hadn't happened.

But Caesar wasn't going to give him time to worry about it – he came up again, rocking the boat with his broad back.

Cranking the motor, Daniel gave distance, keeping his eye on the big croc, as Caesar continued to follow. He was still looking into the sun-glare, and he hadn't even spotted Jen yet.

"Jen! Where the hell are you?"

Her voice came back, strained, "I'm in the cage! I think it's sinking!"

"Where's Quinton?"

"Where do you think?" Jen shouted back. "He's fucking DEAD! Now get me out of this Goddamn cage and let's get the hell out of here!"

Sensible enough, Daniel decided. "Give me a minute!" he hollered, and began to circle the lagoon.

Caesar, however, wasn't having it. Whatever was in the trap, was something he was guarding now. As soon as Daniel started moving towards the tree, the big croc charged.

Cursing, Daniel reversed, holding a steady distance.

This was a territorial animal. It wasn't going to stop.

Daniel took a moment to regret his pistol – he'd had that gun twelve years, and he'd never fired it once – not even at a target.

On the other hand...

He looked down at the harpoon and length of line tied to the bottom of Ol' Bill's boat.

While he was no Ned Land, Daniel HAD thrown a harpoon or two before.

He looked up at the massive craggy back that paced his boat.

Reaching down, he fitted the harpoon to the line.

He knew the technique. He'd caught quite a few gators that way. He even had a couple Nileys under his belt.

Yep. A couple of little six and seven footers – aggressive little sonsofbitches – one of which nearly bit off his hand.

Daniel remembered Quinton hauling one of the feisty little critters in, laughing, "Now imagine pulling out some bugger twice this size – by *hand*."

Quinton had said the thing to remember was that they *were* reptiles – as powerful as they might be, they still operated in bursts.

In between those bursts, there was a lot of leeway.

Quinton had told him that – a world-class trapper – who this particular croc had apparently taken.

Daniel had seen a study that measured a ten-foot croc's bite at two tons.

This one was over six-meters, for sure.

And it was as aggressive an animal as he had ever seen.

Which in this case, actually served to work against it, because, had it not continued to pursue, Daniel might not have got the clean shot with the harpoon that he did.

The big croc seemed to know the harpoon – had probably been on one or two of Ol' Bill's lines before – and when Daniel suddenly stood up, arm raised, it seemed to pause and started to sound.

But Daniel jabbed it in the plates right behind the head, and now he had the big croc on a line.

Really pissed it off too.

With renewed fury, the two-thousand pound beast launched itself at the boat, but Daniel was ready, and reversed hard, pulling the rope taut.

Now the big croc jerked back the other direction, disappearing underwater, trying to pull loose.

Daniel lashed his end to the railing, keeping tension against the boat motor, but letting Caesar pull them along.

The lagoon was probably no more than fifteen-feet at its deepest – maybe a little more after the flooding – otherwise the big animal might have pulled them under. As it was, it simply towed him.

The tension on the rope also allowed Daniel to gauge the big croc's position underwater, and when the line suddenly went slack, he knew it was surfacing again, and reversed, pulling the line tight.

When Caesar's broad back broke the surface, Daniel hit him with a second harpoon, this one attaching to the armored neck. Caesar thrashed in outrage, but Daniel kept tension on both ropes, a game of tug-of-war, never letting the big croc rest.

It was actually a lot like playing a fish... a fish that was larger than your boat, and could maybe come right up on-board and eat you.

Then he heard Jen's voice rising shrilly above the motor.

"Daniel! Hurry! This thing is sinking!"

Daniel glanced over his shoulder and could see the cage listing where its loose pontoon had been torn away. Jen's gap above the water was down to a few inches.

Then it was either go down with the cage or get out into open water.

He had to hurry.

Standing up suddenly in the boat, he threw a third harpoon, again catching the big croc in the neck – and this time it finally did what Daniel had been waiting for, and began to roll.

Doing his best to mimic the way Quinton had done it, Daniel suddenly reversed the motor, dropping the slack in the rope and twirling the line back over the snaggle-toothed snout like a lasso.

The teeth snapped over the rope, rolling, and tangling the jaws shut.

Maybe not as good as Quinton might have done it – a simple roll back would release it – but the trick now was to keep the tension going the other way.

There was a huge splash and a jerk across the stern that threatened to yank the frame of the entire boat apart.

But it seemed, for a moment, that Caesar had begun to tire.

In point of fact, it seemed he was on the retreat, and was towing them in the direction of the tree – likely somewhere close was an underwater den.

It turned out, however, Caesar was headed for the trap itself.

And as Daniel belatedly realized, the big croc had probably been conditioned to treat the cage as sort of a dog-house – a 'horse-trailer' as Abigail had called it – and would go where it felt safe.

Now, tired and feeling threatened, Caesar was trying to get back inside.

Daniel could hear Jen scream as the two-thousand pound monster battened down on the cage. There was the clang of metal as the massive tail crashed down and the pontoon came loose, dropping the cage below the surface.

And Caesar kept fighting.

Sputtering profanity, Daniel pitted the pitiful little twenty-horsepower motor against a ton of pure iron muscle.

Jen had not surfaced. Daniel had seen the tail land several heavy blows across the cage top.

With his options fading quickly, Daniel suddenly reversed the motor again, bringing the boat in close to the tree.

Caesar, who clearly now saw Daniel as an opponent, turned to fight.

Daniel jerked the boat to the right, circling around the Hanging Tree.

Caesar moved to follow – just enough that when Daniel circled back around, the big croc's own weight pulled the line tight around the trunk – like a dog who circles its leash until it becomes stuck with only a few feet.

Daniel motored the boat around the tree twice, securing the line.

Finding himself tethered to a rooted tree rather than a fragile boat, Caesar began to roll again, further tangling his jaws.

Daniel circled a final time, pulling the boat up next to the half-sunken trap.

Cutting the motor, he dived into the murky water.

CHAPTER 24

The trap hung below the surface by its one remaining pontoon and Daniel could see Jen floating limply within.

Feeling his way around to the back of the thirty-foot cage, he found the trap-door, and slipped inside after her.

As he moved, he could *feel* the water displacement, as Caesar rolled and thrashed, just on the other side of the tree.

Below three or four feet, the silt left visibly at near zero – his hands found her before his eyes did.

She was utterly limp – unresponsive.

He grabbed her and pulled her to the surface.

In a single motion, he dragged the both of them up on top of the remaining pontoon and laid her on her back.

She had taken a vicious blow across the head – one of the cage bars – probably when the tail came down – splitting her scalp at the hairline, bleeding into her blond hair, and swelling lumpish and purple.

He found a steady pulse.

But she wasn't breathing.

In the awkward space on the bobbing pontoon, Daniel picked her up and tossed her over his shoulder like an infant, and she vomited swamp water.

He lay her back and began resuscitation. He did so professionally – he was a qualified paramedic – and he had no doubt he'd get her started again.

Absolutely none.

He would NOT ALLOW himself the slightest doubt.

And he kept at it, even as Caesar seemed to have finally figured the right direction and was now rolling his jaws free of the tangling rope.

Daniel breathed for her – at one point, she vomited a little more water into his mouth.

Behind him, Caesar's jaws were now loose, and the big croc strained against the line that still wrapped it around the thick trunk.

But just like the jaw rope, as soon as it stopped resisting and simply followed the restraining rope back around, and it would be free.

For the moment, its own stubbornness worked against it and, instead, it strained against the line.

Daniel darted longingly towards the boat. But he needed the pontoon's flat surface to work.

Caesar's jaws had found one of the restraining lines – the second one Daniel had sunk into his back – and the cord snapped loudly.

Daniel shut his eyes, breathing. Breathing.

"Come on, Jen," he whispered, as he breathed into her mouth.

He felt the first tremor of doubt. And with it the first chill of despair.

"Please..." and through his professional, mechanical breaths, he choked for just a second.

Just as Jen herself choked up another glut of water, and finally gasped a breath on her own.

Daniel turned her over on her side, letting the remaining fluid vomit itself out.

She still lulled unconscious, but she was breathing again.

He had just sat her up, when the rope around the tree behind him suddenly broke, snapping back at him like a whip.

Daniel turned to see Caesar pulling back from the trunk, both remaining harpoon lines trailing like kite-tails – anchored to nothing – and, of course, its jaws now free.

Sonofabitch. It didn't even *need* to figure out the angles – brute force was enough.

Grabbing Jen up in his arms, Daniel scurried onto the boat – which was still attached to the tree by its end of the broken line.

Just on the other side of the tree, Caesar's craggy, knobbed back turned in their direction.

Dropping Jen at his feet, Daniel cut the line, pushing away from the tree, and cranked the motor.

It sputtered once but didn't fire.

"Oh, fuck this," Daniel hissed, yanking the rope one more time.

In the leisurely manner of crocs, Caesar circled the tree and, even as the motor fired to life, Daniel realized it had cornered them between the trunk and the trap.

As if sensing advantage, Caesar actually seemed to pause – savoring.

Daniel tensed – options were limited. He would simply have to try and motor past – if it caught hold of them this time, it would simply tear the boat apart.

Then...?

Daniel looked at his pocketknife.

Well, he'd go for the bastard's eyes, if it came to that.

He revved the motor.

Caesar held steady, as if waiting for Daniel to make his move.

In the non-silence of the swamp, the moment seemed to hang.

The sound of the gunshot was as startling as the sudden cry of a banshee.

There was a second shot, and then a third – suppressed pops, as if with a silencer.

In the water in front of him, Caesar suddenly bucked, and thrashed, disappearing underwater in an angry splash.

Daniel turned to see Abigail standing in her rowboat – silent as a predator, her rifle raised to one shoulder.

Caesar reappeared at the surface several yards away, the craggy back breaking water like a miniature island.

Abigail fired again.

A flowered dart appeared on the croc's neck, and Daniel realized there were three others, clustered all around the head.

Caesar still moved lazily, but now suddenly appeared stoned.

Abigail sat the rifle aside, nodding to Daniel.

"That ought to do it," she said.

She rowed over to where the tow rope still trailed loosely, attached to Caesar's neck. She gaffed the line, pulling herself along until she sat right up next to the floating croc.

"Tranquilizer darts?" Daniel asked.

"Ol' Bill kept a few around the house."

"You aren't going to kill it?"

Abigail shook her head. "That croc's worth a lot of money to me alive. A whole new life."

"Jen's hurt," Daniel said. "We've got to get help."

He held up his phone. He had never charged it last night and he found it dead.

Abigail held up her one. "Mine's cheap. I can't get a signal." She nodded up river. "We can get online at my cabin."

Then she pulled her rowboat up beside the cage. "Here, help me with this pontoon."

"Why?"

"So we can get Caesar back in his cage and take him home with us." Daniel started to object but she cut him off with a look. "Then it will all be over," she said.

Abigail pulled up next to the half-sunken trap and started pulling. "Come on. Help me."

After a few minutes, they managed to get the pontoon lashed back into position – still dragging, but floatable.

Behind them, Caesar drifted apathetically – not resisting as Abigail took up the harpoon line and began to reel him in. After a moment,

Daniel stepped in to help, guiding the big semi-conscious croc into the cage.

Abigail dropped the hatch door shut.

"Let's go," she said.

Inside the cage, Caesar blinked lazily.

CHAPTER 25

Jen was still unconscious, and Daniel was beginning to worry.

Abandoning her rowboat at the Tree, Abigail had taken over the motor, while Daniel did his best to dress Jen's injuries.

She was breathing, and her pulse was steady, but she had not yet stirred.

Daniel grit his teeth at their slow pace. He was debating simply cutting the cage loose – whether he had to throw Abigail out of the boat to do it, or not – but he was also aware she had the only working phone, and could call for life-flight the moment she got a signal – and the closest available spot for a helicopter to land was her cabin.

And they *had* Caesar – they couldn't risk the big croc getting away.

Although they *could* just shoot it.

Abigail watched him mildly, perhaps guessing his train of thought.

"Take a breath, Ranger," she said. "We aren't going to get there any faster."

Daniel stepped on a moment of temper, and did take a breath.

She was right – they could cut the cage loose and still be dragging a meandering path through the glades, and not save fifteen minutes.

And if that fifteen minutes was the difference for Jen?

Daniel grit his teeth.

But the truth was, Abigail was moving them along just fine. The cage was an easy tow, and they weren't burdened by the little motor on his own parks boat.

The truth was, he was not a trained paramedic right now.

He forced himself to calm down.

"Easy," he murmured aloud, rubbing the crusted blood from Jen's forehead, where he had bandaged that nasty gash.

It seemed forever before Ol' Bill's cabin finally came into view.

Daniel glanced back. "Haven't you got a damn signal yet?"

Abigail checked her phone. "Not yet."

Excruciatingly slowly, moving against the current they puttered up to the floating dock.

The moment they touched down, Daniel vaulted over the side, and went running for the cabin, pounding up the stairs to the back deck.

He took momentary note that the door was open – in fact, looked *kicked* open – when he was suddenly met in the face by the butt of a shotgun.

Daniel had taken a good punch in his day and was, in fact, known as a fairly sturdy fellow – thus, it took a second blow – a pretty damned hard one – to put him down.

In bleary semi-consciousness, he heard Quinton Marvin's thick backwater growl.

"Stay down, son. I ain't got no problem with you. Don't give me no cause to."

Daniel struggled to rise – fully intending to give him cause – but could not quite find his feet.

Quinton sighed, this time simply letting go a hard right hook, and Daniel finally dropped.

Standing on the dock, Abigail shouldered her rifle.

Leaving Daniel where he'd fallen, Quinton made his way down the stairs.

They stood facing each other. Quinton still had the shotgun at his side – one of Ol' Bill's stash – pilfered from the house – probably under the bed. He let it hang loosely.

Abigail's rifle was business-end up.

"I thought you were dead," Abigail said.

"I thought I was too," Quinton replied. "I woke up in a hole. Crawled out, and here I was."

He nodded under the cabin.

"That's the lair," he said. "Under the cabin all along."

Quinton shrugged. "And why wouldn't it be? That's where he'd been getting fed for the last forty years. It came where it got food, warmth."

The old trapper shook his head.

"He had a damned heat-lamp down there."

Quinton's eyes narrowed.

"You knew it was there all along, didn't you, Abigail?" he said. "That's why you put that big trap closest to the cabin."

"I thought that might be the one," Abigail allowed.

She shrugged. "I didn't know about the heat-lamp," she said. "That's new. Ol' Bill upgraded a lot."

"You could've caught that big ol' croc at any time."

"I had some things I needed to do," Abigail said. "Easier if it's out on the water."

This time when he spoke, the old trapper's voice cracked just a little bit.

"He had my boy down there, Abigail. I woke up and he was lying next to me. All slimy-white like a rotting fish."

There was a heartbeat of silence.

Abigail remained unmoved, her rifle unwavering.

Quinton stared down the barrel dangerously.

"By my count," he said, "that's the third son I've lost to that damn animal and your goddamned family."

Now he raised his own shotgun.

"Get out of my way, Abigail." He pumped both shells into place. "I've got two shots, but I'll shoot you twice and reload before I let that croc live one more day."

Behind him on the dock, Daniel had heard this last, and even as he struggled to rise, he actually found himself feeling a moment of pure human sympathy for the old bastard.

Daniel looked at him, covered in mud, the semi-crazed look in his eyes – and he tried to imagine what it would have been like waking up in that hole. He had heard about it happening – Africans taken by Nileys – one gentleman had come-to with the croc sleeping beside him – he'd had to crawl past it, slipping out of the tunneled lair into utterly black water.

Then imagine waking up in a reptilian larder of bones and stinking meat – and seeing your SON?

He wondered who else's bones might be buried down in that den, somewhere right under their feet? Perhaps the odd fisherman or two – along with people Ol' Bill didn't like.

And perhaps a few Abigail hadn't liked as well.

Any burgeoning sympathy, however, would have to wait. With Quinton's attention on Abigail, Daniel moved from the ground, crawling towards the stairs.

Unfortunately, he was still wobbly, and he stumbled on the first step, and all he managed to do was tumble to the bottom, almost at Quinton's feet – his efforts earning him another hard shotgun butt across the head, this one opening a divot across his scalp and knocking him back into semi-consciousness.

"Goddamnit," Quinton said. "Crocs have been snappin' at me for fifty years – you ain't catching me like that. Now, you just sit tight. This ain't none of your business."

He turned to Abigail.

"I told you to get out of my way," he said.

Abigail shook her head mildly.

"You may not be in it for the money," she replied. "I am."

She nodded over her shoulder. "My trap. My property. My catch."

"Money ain't everything," Quinton said. "Sometimes there're principals."

Abigail responded with polite laughter.

"Don't believe in principals?" Quinton asked.

Abigail's eyes narrowed.

"I *know*, Quinton," she said. "I know you killed my father."

"And how exactly would you know anything about that?"

"From your son," Abigail said. "Pete told me."

Quinton frowned. "When did you talk to Pete?"

"Never mind, Pete. It's true, isn't it? You killed him."

Quinton did a slow burn.

"Does it surprise you?" he said finally. "That your daddy didn't die in any accident? Maybe you should be asking 'why now?' Why not a long time ago?"

Quinton spat. "After what he'd done? I gotta tell ya, there's been many a night I sat out here – just watching..."

He let the implication hang. There was no doubt, anyway.

"When the time came that it had to be done, the powers-that-be did me the honor." Quinton shrugged. "Besides, your dad was a tough old bastard. I was probably the only one that could have got the drop on him without getting fed to his damned croc myself. A lot of others had tried."

His eyes narrowed.

"But you know that, don't you girl? You grew up knowing that."

He spat again. And now he began to walk forward.

"It don't matter anyhow," he said. "I'm gonna kill that animal, just like I killed your daddy.

I'm sorry enough, but it had to be done. Time was 'he needed killing' was a valid defense."

Abigail smiled, leveling her aim between his eyes.

"Still is," she said.

Quinton was shaking his head, not stopping.

"Yeah," he said, "I killed your daddy. And I'd do it again tomorrow. The miserable sonofabitch didn't deserve to live."

Now his calm voice finally boiled over.

"Goddamnit, girl. If your daddy hadn't stolen and raped your mother, you might be my granddaughter."

He stood not five feet in front of her, looking down her rifle.

"You don't know what happened, do you?" he said. "The night your mamma died?"

"She fell in with the gators."

"Not the gators," Quinton said. He pointed to the cage behind her. "That bloody-damn croc. Johnny told me. Ol' Bill – he could have saved her. He had his rifle in his hand. He came out to use it on my son – took a shot at him – that's how she fell in – the river, not the pond."

Quinton nodded. "Makes more sense, doesn't it? How the hell would she have gotten in the pond? Running to the river?

"And that big croc was waiting for her. But your daddy, he wouldn't fire nothing but 'warning shots'."

And now Quinton took another step forward.

"He just didn't want to kill the fuckin' crocodile."

Abigail blinked once.

"Yeah," she said, "he always did love those crocs."

"That animal killed your mother, Abigail."

There was a tick of silence. For just a split second, Abigail shut her eyes...

... and in that single moment, the croc will move...

Just like a croc, Quinton moved, reaching for the barrel of her gun.

Lying where he had fallen, Daniel was not sure which came first – that forward moment, or the blast of Abigail's rifle.

She shot him – dead in the chest.

The impact flipped him over backwards like a horse-kick.

He toppled over into the water. Daniel heard a small, unimportant-sounding splash.

Abigail's eyes shut again, her face utterly calm – and Daniel, blinking off the effects of a near-concussion knockout blow, was not a hundred-percent sure what he saw – and would forever wonder at that seeming blink of inattention that had caused Quinton to reach for her.

OR had he reached out once he saw her begin to squeeze the trigger?

In either case, despite holding a gun on her, he had moved in with his hands.

Abigail hadn't been so restrained.

Now she glanced impassively where the water still rippled.

Then she turned back to where Caesar lay, his lazy eye watching – perhaps even perceiving.

Did it recognize the slim figure standing on the dock? Did it know Abigail?

It had grown up here, after all – Daniel remembered the story of a big saltie that had finally nabbed a family dog who had lived along its stretch of beach for years.

In this case, Caesar was the dog.

Abigail stood, looking contemplatively at the monster in the cage.

This spider had woven her web well – Daniel watched for a moment, wondering whether the big croc would follow Quinton.

It also occurred to Daniel that *he* was a witness as well.

Was the same thought occurring to Abigail?

She stood, head bowed, looking out at the massive cage floating in the water.

Her face was utterly blank – like a doll – with those black eyes – that bottomless depth.

Daniel heard her whisper.

"He really did love those crocs."

Then she tossed her rifle on its strap over her shoulder, turned and began walking towards him, casual as a public beach on a sunny day.

"Well," she said, eyeing Daniel meaningfully, "I guess we're done here."

He tensed as she reached into her hip pocket... and pulled out her phone.

"Here," she said. "I got a signal now. Better call your chopper."

CHAPTER 26

By the time the chopper arrived, Jen had achieved a bleary semi-consciousness – enough to recognize Daniel tending to her – enough to ask what happened to his face.

Daniel had actually forgotten his own face had taken multiple blows, and probably looked a sight. He actually laughed.

The chopper had landed in the front lot beside the garage, and now the paramedics had Jen trussed up on a gurney.

As they brought her out on the dock, one of them noticed the twenty-foot crocodile floating stuporously in a half-demolished cage almost right next to them. He looked up at Daniel.

"You're going to have to tell me *this* story," he said.

Within minutes they had Jen prepped for flight. The man who had spoken before turned to Daniel.

"We're going to take her now, sir. You can meet her at the hospital." And then, seeing the look in Daniel's eyes, gave him a pat on the arm. "She's going to be fine."

Daniel kneeled down where Jen lay on the stretcher. She blinked up at him, gripping his hand. He smiled. "Hear that? You're going to be fine."

He gave her hand a squeeze... and it was decidedly not brotherly. She squeezed back.

"I'll catch up with you," he said.

As they loaded up, trundling past the gator pond, Daniel heard one of the paramedics, "What the hell IS this place?"

If they only knew.

Daniel turned to where Abigail had been sitting, silently and unobtrusively.

Behind her, Caesar also sat peacefully enough.

"You need to go after her," Abigail said.

Daniel nodded.

"What do ya' say, Ranger?" she said. "You think your croc park could use a twenty-footer?"

Daniel nodded again. "I imagine so."

She met his eyes levelly. "Let's be clear, here. I expect to be well-compensated. Quinton wanted to put out for bid. Tell your Mr. Wesley I could do that too."

"I don't expect that to be a problem," Daniel said. "As far as Wesley is concerned, I think you can fairly name your price."

Daniel cleared his voice uncomfortably. "There are still going to be official statements. You're going to need to talk to the cops."

"You mean, ol' Sheriff Barnes?"

Daniel smiled thinly. "Probably a little higher than Barnes."

"So?" she said. "What are you going to tell them?"

Abigail smiled as she spoke – that same indulgent smile from when he pretended he wasn't going to spend the night with her.

"I guess it's pretty clear-cut self-defense," Daniel said. "Isn't it?"

Her gun on her shoulder – Abigail stepped forward into his arms, just as she had at the cabin.

And once again, Daniel let her.

She kissed him softly – slowly, letting her lips trail down his neck – her teeth touching lightly – just over the jugular – the loving touch of a fang dripped with poison.

Then she stepped back.

"Be seeing you, Ranger."

Her striking green eyes blinked – intelligence untouched by conscience – yet nevertheless, full of all other human wants and desires. A true human id.

If threatened, it would defend itself savagely – unbound by any morality that extended beyond meeting an opposing force.

The rough justice of the primordial swamp.

Abigail WAS the swamp.

Daniel had held this prickly spider – the deadly mate-devouring female – close to his breast – he had stroked her hair, as he had seen an entomologist stroke the smooth hair of a tarantula, as it had postured like a cat, accepting the pleasurable caress.

But the moment there was a perception of a threat...?

Or Ol' Bill's criteria? Folks who did him wrong?

Or folks he HAD to.

A wavering of trust, and Daniel could see himself hand-fed, limb-by-dismembered-limb into the gator pond. She would do it with the same expression she had when she gave them chickens.

"Take care of yourself, Abigail," he said.

Abigail stood on the dock, watching him as he loaded up his truck, and left her behind.

In the trap behind her, Caesar watched.

CHAPTER 27

To much fanfare, 'King Caesar' the giant, man-eating crocodile was introduced to the public – billed by Gator Glades as the largest croc ever measured – just over twenty-two-feet, and well over two-thousand pounds.

The local press leaped on the story – the drama of its capture – the size of the monster. A documentary had already been put together and a movie was on the way.

Daniel had been as good as his word, and had made sure Abigail got her money. Robert Wesley had made her a substantial offer, intending to silence any on-line bidders – and he did so characterizing her as a hero to the press.

Not only that, but Wesley also arranged for the state to finally buy away the property she had inherited from her father, so it could be absorbed into the protected lands. Daniel did not know the actual numbers there, but the papers had been signed and he suspected Abigail had walked away quite comfortable.

She had attended the grand-opening for 'King Caesar', and had met Wesley himself – Daniel had introduced them, and Wesley had graciously thanked her.

"I knew your father," he told her.

Abigail's green-eyes flashed just a touch darker.

"Did you?" she said. But her smile never faded, and she shook Wesley's hand agreeably.

Daniel had looked at her oddly, then. But he had stopped asking questions.

There had been a certain amount of official red-tape – Sheriff Barnes had actually been right on top of it, coordinating quickly with the state cops, and had already put a bulletin out for any lingering hired-hands in Quinton's employ.

"Been expecting something like this for a long time," he told Daniel. "And I did tell you to watch yourself out there, didn't I?" The rustic old lawman shook his head. "No one ever listens."

Barnes had also taken Abigail aside and advised her to be careful.

"Ol' Quinton's youngest boy, Pete, ain't turned up yet," he said. "You need to watch yourself until we round him up."

Abigail had smiled gratefully. "I will, Sheriff," she said.

Those dark eyes flashed briefly at Daniel, who had frowned, but said nothing.

As far as he knew, no-one was looking in the gator pond yet. Fifty, maybe a hundred alligators? And maybe a few baby crocs?

Daniel had a hunch no one was ever going to find a trace of Pete. Or any of the 'lingering hired hands'.

His mind was on a tally he was deliberately NOT running in his head.

He had other things to worry about – for example, the side of the story that was currently being suppressed – as Wesley and his publicist's hat had arranged – yes, they had caught two big crocs – but there was a potential generation still waiting out on the water.

Growing. With hybrid vigor.

In the following weeks, Daniel would be leading crews back out on the water, searching the protected areas – all the best hiding places for deliberately-planted invaders.

He was not looking forward to any of it.

But for today, Jen was waiting back at the hospital. She was scheduled to go home, and Daniel was going there now to pick her up.

Wesley had clapped an encouraging hand on Daniel's back. "You're a good man, Reid," Wesley said. "Tell Jen we're looking forward to having her back."

Abigail had followed him to the gate, just under the giant croc jaws that led the public down its gullet.

She bid him goodbye more formally this time – with a handshake.

"Take care, Ranger," she said.

CHAPTER 28

The crowds had finally gone home and Gator Glades had grown dark.

Alone in his tank, Caesar sat motionless, as he had all day.

The big croc was aware of its surroundings – absorbing it all as placidly as ever – filtering all input under the simple equation of food-versus-threat.

It didn't like the crowds of hominids that had gathered around its tank all day, but neither was it bothered by them – Caesar was used to humans.

In point of fact, he was eyeing each and every one of them as a potential mouthful should any just get close enough.

But then the crowd left and night had fallen.

And somewhere in the middle of the night, a lone figure stole onto the property.

Caesar was aware of the movement – and recognized it.

After a moment, the trespasser stepped into the light.

Abigail stared down into the pool.

She and Caesar regarded each other – old siblings – raised together.

Abigail wondered if Caesar ever felt jealous after she had come along – like an older brother missing the attention of his parents.

For her part, Abigail could relate to the little sister living in her big brother's shadow. There was, after all, never doubting priorities.

She understood about her life now. As well as what happened to her father.

It was the fisherman. And the little girl.

Ol' Bill had let his crocs out – and that made him a liability. It brought unwanted attention to the larger operation.

It was just business. Ol' Bill was supply-side – right on the edge of the biggest private breeding ground in the country.

It also explained why Quinton had never taken Ol' Bill out until now – he and his boys were the round-up.

But Ol' Bill had... appetites. And occasionally needed to be covered for.

It was the attack on the fisherman that broke the camel's back – on film, right out in front of God and everybody. And the powers-that-be knew where the trail would lead once the croc was finally caught.

Ol' Bill, naturally, would ask for help – and the powers decided they'd had enough.

So they sent Quinton out to club him and drop him in the swamp.

The fact that Nemo ate him was sheer coincidence.

She'd gotten THAT much from Pete that day.

Now there were just a few loose ends.

Caesar stood blinking up at her out of his pool – no doubt gauging the distance – measuring for that moment she stepped into range – and waiting for that moment of inattention.

Abigail pulled the rifle off her shoulder and fired two shots right between the croc's big blinking eyes – just as she had between Nemo's only a few short weeks before.

Caesar kicked, his massive tail thrashing, as the twenty-foot beast convulsed and flipped in the water.

Then, with a quivering shudder, the big croc fell limp, and lay still.

Abigail stared down, eyes slitted like a cat's.

"Yeah," she said, "he really did love those crocs."

Pulling her hood back over her head, Abigail hopped back over the fence, and left the park behind.

She had dutifully researched her route – locations of security cameras, etc. – and she made her way to the little pickup anonymously parked less than a mile away – an old farm vehicle she had wire-started out of some random garage – and would take her to the dock where she had a boat waiting.

Pete's boat – which she would arrange to be found floating somewhere deep in the 'glades.

She had a little refuse she needed to take out onto the water.

Packed discreetly within a large cooler on the back of the little outboard, was Councilman Wesley.

Abigail had gotten part of the story from Pete. The rest she had simply gotten online in her father's records – payments from Robert Wesley – e-mails – even legal and medical bills. All covered by Robert Wesley.

Probably they had figured the circumstantial evidence would be enough to finger Ol' Bill as just a wild swamp-crazy – a lone actor.

They hadn't counted on Abigail.

She left the old pickup parked on the dock. Leaving the boat motor off, preserving the early-morning silence, she pushed off, paddling out into the current, making certain her packed meat-case was securely lashed to the bow.

All routine.

Abigail wasn't like her father – she didn't get-off on it – she didn't THINK of reasons.

But she'd done it enough to get good at it.

And it WAS a bit habit-forming.

And now she cast a dire eye at the cooler that contained the mortal remains of Councilman Wesley.

Truth to tell, she had thought about feeding him to his fucking crocodile.

But, as poetically satisfying as that might be, there was no need to draw any arrows for the authorities. If anything was going to cough up a little bit of Robert Wesley, Abigail preferred it be deep out on the water.

After all, the swamp never gave up its dead.

But sometimes its denizens did.

THE END

SEVEREDPRESS

CHECK OUT OTHER GREAT HORROR NOVELS

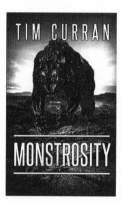

MONSTROSITY
by Tim Curran

The Food. It seeped from the ground, a living, gushing, teratogenic nightmare. It contaminated anything that ate it, causing nature to run wild with horrible mutations, creating massive monstrosities that roam the land destroying towns and cities, feeding on livestock and human beings and one another. Now Frank Bowman, an ordinary farmer with no military skills, must get his children to safety. And that will mean a trip through the contaminated zone of monsters, madmen, and The Food itself. Only a fool would attempt it. Or a man with a mission.

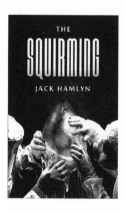

THE SQUIRMING
by Jack Hamlyn

You are their hosts

You are their food

The parasites came out of nowhere, squirming horrors that enslaved the human race. They turned the population into mindless pack animals, psychotic cannibalistic hordes whose only purpose was to feed them.

Now with the human race teetering at the edge of extinction, extermination teams are fighting back, killing off the parasites and their voracious hosts. Taking them out one by one in violent, bloody encounters.

The future of mankind is at stake.

And time is running out

CHECK OUT OTHER GREAT HORROR NOVELS

DEATH CRAWLERS
by Gerry Griffiths

Worldwide, there are thought to be 8,000 species of centipede, of which, only 3,000 have been scientifically recorded. The venom of Scolopendra gigantea—the largest of the arthropod genus found in the Amazon rainforest—is so potent that it is fatal to small animals and toxic to humans. But when a cargo plane departs the Amazon region and crashes inside a national park in the United States, much larger and deadlier creatures escape the wreckage to roam wild, reproducing at an astounding rate. Entomologist, Frank Travis solicits small town sheriff Wanda Rafferty's help and together they investigate the crash site. But as a rash of gruesome deaths befalls the townsfolk of Prospect, Frank and Wanda will soon discover how vicious and cunning these new breed of predators can be. Meanwhile, Jake and Nora Carver, and another backpacking couple, are venturing up into the mountainous terrain of the park. If only they knew their fun-filled weekend is about to become a living nightmare.

THE PULLER
by Michael Hodges

Matt Kearns has two choices: fight or hide. The creature in the orchard took the rest. Three days ago, he arrived at his favorite place in the world, a remote shack in Michigan's Upper Peninsula. The plan was to mourn his father's death and figure out his life. Now he's fighting for it. An invisible creature has him trapped. Every time Matt tries to flee, he's dragged backwards by an unseen force. Alone and with no hope of rescue, Matt must escape the Puller's reach. But how do you free yourself from something you cannot see?

Made in the USA
Middletown, DE
17 June 2019